The Christmas Cruise

by

Barbara Lohr

Purple Egret Press
Savannah, Georgia 31411

This book is a work of fiction. The characters, events and places in the book are products of the author's imagination and are either fictitious or used fictitiously. Any similarity of real persons, living or dead, is purely coincidental and not intended by the author.

ISBN: 978-1-945523-27-4

For my husband Ted,

with wonderful memories

of the Danube.

Chapter 1

"Should we spend Christmas Eve with your parents or mine?" Hadley opened the calendar on her phone.

"Christmas Eve?" Brock said in that absent-minded way he had when he was thinking of three things at once.

The theme song from the Charlie Brown Christmas show played overhead in the Signature Room. Meeting for a quick lunch, Hadley was taking her fiancé through their holiday plans. Thank goodness Brock had been able to break away from work. The view of Chicago from the ninety-fifth floor was spectacular during the holidays.

"We should settle our plans for the holidays. I've been so busy tying up loose ends on this South Shore deal. But my mother wants to know and so does yours." When she tapped her fingers on the table, her engagement ring caught the light. Hadley smiled, enjoying the sparkle. The ring was outrageous. Might take a while to pay for it, but this three-carat stone was so worth it. *Only six months until the wedding.*

But back to business. "We could split the time, I suppose. You know, spend an hour with my family and then drive across the city to yours. Do the reverse on Christmas Day."

Brock groaned. "Are you kidding me? In Chicago traffic? Driving from Winnetka to Glen Ellyn could take at least an hour. Traffic would be bumper to bumper."

"Okay. Good point." The young mother at the next table was trying to handle a little boy and an infant. She really had her hands full. The older boy began thumping a spoon on the high chair tray. Looking like she was at her wits end, the woman handed the boy a breadstick.

Now, where were we? "So what should we do?"

"About the time with your family." Brock shifted in his chair and the waitress arrived with their lunch. Salmon for her and seabass for Brock. They both were sensible eaters. Brock encouraged her to watch her weight and he was so right. But what was this? A juicy grilled burger covered with swiss cheese sat in front of her fiancé. It looked disgustingly wonderful. She hadn't eaten one in a long time.

"Sorry, but there's been a mistake," she told the waitress. Brock had placed their order before she arrived but he never would have ordered this.

"No mistake. Thank you." Brock waved the waitress away and grabbed the ketchup.

Hadley was still staring at the burger. "If you eat that, you'll want to curl up and nap."

"I decided to get what I want for a change." Lifting the top of his bun, he squeezed ketchup over the melted swiss cheese. His chin was set in *that way*. End of discussion.

All right then. And what did he mean by that comment? "For a change?"

He took a big bite.

Hadley broke off a chunk of her salmon with a fork. "After the holidays, there will probably be a whole bunch of showers for us. I heard a rumor about a couple's shower in February. Jack and Rene. You know, out in Naperville?"

"A couple's shower?" he mumbled around a mouthful. One of children at the next table squealed. Brock cringed.

"Right. Remember the one for Marla and Jared last year?"

Nodding, Brock chewed and swallowed. "The guys ended up playing poker in the family room while the women opened gifts upstairs. That one?"

"Yes, I guess." Was that how he saw it? "Anyway, we have a lot to look forward to. My wedding dress will be in." Hadley could hardly wait. That Vera Wang design was to die for.

Head bowed, Brock kept eating that darn burger.

While her toddler scattered breadstick crumbs onto the floor, the young mother was trying to nurse her infant. She reminded Hadley of her sister Leanne. She'd nursed both her children and was expecting again.

"Sorry, maybe I should have asked for another table. I know you're not comfortable around little kids."

Now, he cleared his throat. "That's the problem, Hadley. Well, one of them."

"Could I top off your iced tea?" The waitress had circled back with a pitcher.

"Yes, please," Brock said and Hadley nodded. *What problem?*

"Now what were you saying?" she asked after the waitress had left. Overhead "Jingle Bell Rock" was playing and Hadley jiggled one foot.

What was going on with him? The man hadn't even asked what she wanted for Christmas. But Brock always liked to surprise her. Maybe he'd whip out a little tennis bracelet. Of course, she'd have to take it back. That simply wasn't in their budget, not with all the upcoming wedding expenses.

Of course, she'd spent tons of time searching for Christmas gifts for him. Her closets were full of carefully wrapped gifts. For months she'd been clicking on sales, from Prime Day to Black Friday. One of her favorite gifts for him was a gold keychain with a heart engraved with their entwined initials. She was keeping her last name and he hadn't seemed to mind.

"Hadley, I want to take a break."

"Really? It's the middle of the day." Did he have something romantic in mind? Maybe he wanted to go Christmas shopping together. But that wouldn't be like him.

She watched his throat move as he swallowed. Brock looked out at the city below. "Things are moving too fast. We talked about the wedding and the showers. But we haven't talked about some of the other stuff."

"What other stuff? Are you feeling okay?" He wasn't making sense.

Brock wasn't smiling. "The kids."

"Kids? Are you talking about our children? The children we'll have?"

The glum look on his face gave her the answer. Had he forgotten? "I think we said we wanted a big family, didn't we? I mean, I come from a big family. And we're both so successful. We'll have plenty of resources…"

"No, I think *you* said you wanted a big family. I tried to consider that. Really I did, Hadley." His eyes darted to the next table where the little boy was now tossing whole bread sticks onto the floor. Oh my gosh, she wanted to run over and help that poor mother.

A corner table might've been better for this conversation. But Hadley hadn't seen this coming. And today she'd wanted this view. "Of course, *our* children will be better behaved."

Brock snorted. "Like Kevin's?"

Now, that touched a nerve. "I don't like the way you're talking about my brother's three little boys." Okay, they were a handful. But children grew out of those phases, didn't they? Kevin had.

"That's just it. I don't think I want children. I'm sorry, Hadley, but I'm an only child. When I think about Christmas, I can't take that chaos again. It's a circus at your house."

Circus? She would have felt offended. But what he was saying had a kernel of truth. Christmas could be crazy. Crazy and fun. And the Parker family liked it that way.

"Let's take a break and think about this." He wouldn't look at her. "I don't want to hurt you, Hadley, but I think we need time."

"So, if we weren't planning on a family, then everything would be fine?" What was he saying? Reaching for one of his french fries, she bit off an end. They were cold and disgusting.

"Maybe. Probably." Clearing his throat, Brock pushed his plate aside. "We're both professionals with successful careers. The world could be our oyster."

"Yes. Sure. It *is*." What Brock was saying was true. In his position with a law firm specializing in utilities and banks, he'd been pulling down six figures for a long time. For a guy in his mid-thirties, he was doing well. Same with Hadley, although she was a bit younger. People always told her she was "driven." With the help of her assistant Miranda, she worked long hours in commercial real estate and hoped to close on another converted mall before Christmas.

Now the down payments they'd made spun through her mind like an unending receipt. The reception at his parents' private club. The photographers—still and video—the classical quartet for the church, the rock band for the reception. Planning and paying for this wedding would be no problem. No way was she going to put all this on her parents. They'd agreed. But if they canceled?

Was she hyperventilating? Then there were the personal gifts. Not only had she purchased the bridesmaid gifts for six women, she'd also ordered Brock's groomsmen gifts. He'd been so busy. So stressed out.

Bingo. Maybe that was it. "Are you having a really bad week?"

Into his silence poured the carol "God Rest Ye Merry Gentlemen." The holidays suddenly felt distant. Unattainable. Hadley's hands began to shake. She set her fork down.

"Have your feelings for me changed? Is that what you're saying?"

Brock still hunched over his plate.

"I thought we were on the same page with this. Why, we're way into our wedding plans."

When he swung his head up, she almost felt sorry for him. The man looked so confused. "I do love you. But I just don't know..." Taking her hands, he brushed a thumb over her knuckles. "Maybe I am stressed." His grip loosened. "I...we need time to think." With that he slid another glance to the children at the next table. A waitress was sweeping up the breadcrumbs.

Hadley's mouth felt dry and she took a sip of her iced tea. "Maybe we do need a holiday break." But Hadley shrank inside. The parties, the gatherings, New Year's Eve. They would be the main topic of conversation. Brad and Angelina. Kanye and Kim. Brock and Hadley.

If only Brock didn't look so perfect today in his navy blue blazer and oxford cloth shirt. The red and green striped tie was perfect for the holidays. For two years Brock Phillips had been the man of her dreams. Walking down the aisle with him became her goal. Now she had to regroup. Reassess. Hadn't she taken that three-hour seminar last month about being flexible to close a sale? Miranda had her notes somewhere.

Hadley patted his hand. "Don't worry about it. Let's uncouple for a while. Take a break. Looks like we both have some thinking to do." That may have sounded calm and logical, and she wished she felt that way. But what were her options?

Maybe she should think about the family thing. She did business with some childless couples who led wonderful lives. Cynthia and Rex traveled a lot. Owned two homes. Marie and

Noah had pedigreed poodles they talked about all the time.

Had she assumed that she could have all that—a great, two-income life and a family too? Her sister Leanne didn't work and they only had two kids, Amber and Stewart, with one more on the way. Had their standard of living taken a nosedive with each child? Probably. Steve was a high school teacher. They called this baby their "summer break."

Brock took care of the check and somehow she made it out of that restaurant. When they said goodbye, he hugged Hadley and kissed her cheek. A frigid breeze from Lake Michigan blew as she turned toward the parking garage. Although she'd planned on shopping for her nephews and niece at the FAO Schwarz toy store, she didn't have the heart for it anymore. Maybe she'd skip the office and work from her condo that afternoon. She felt a headache throbbing behind her eyes. On the way home, "Have Yourself a Merry Little Christmas" was playing on the radio. She turned it off.

***

"You and Brock are going on a break? What does that mean? Are you taking a trip?" Her face flushed from stirring the gravy, Hadley's mother frowned. It was Sunday and they were in the kitchen. Hadley was helping her mother get dinner ready. Opening the oven, she reached for a baked potato.

"Oh! Darn!" She'd forgotten the hot pads. Dashing to the sink, she ran cold water over her hand. Her fingers still pulsed with pain. "We're not going *on* a break. We're *taking* a break. There's a difference."

Her mother blinked. "I don't get it." Lifting the gravy whisk, Mom stopped stirring. Brown drops hit the kitchen tile.

"Mom, you're dripping gravy everywhere."

After that disastrous lunch with Brock, she'd written down some talking points for her parents. Now she couldn't remember a single word. "I think he's just nervous. Hectic job and all that."

As if Hadley herself didn't have enough to worry about with that upcoming sale of South Shore Enterprises. If that went through, she wouldn't have to worry so much about the money she could lose if they canceled. "We're thinking things over."

Mom tilted her head to one side. "Really, sweetheart? That sure sounds like you're calling it quits." By this time her mother was whispering. The whisk had been forgotten on the kitchen counter. She ran both hands down the front of her red Christmas apron with Margie stitched across the top. If the family heard this conversation, they'd flip out. Her brother Kevin had never taken to Brock.

"I'm so sorry. That man." Grabbing a paper towel, Mom handed it to Hadley. She stooped and wiped up the gravy. Her mother made the best gravy ever. Brock always said so. But really, didn't gravy occlude people's arteries? Why worry about that when her fiancé was now wolfing down greasy burgers?

Her eyes burned. For the past few days, she'd been holding it together. Getting her ducks lined up, as Mom would say. Over the holidays, she'd take some time off. Walk down Michigan Avenue and meditate. Well, that would never work. All she'd see on the Magnificent Mile, as it was called, was one gorgeous window after another. Things she could buy for her new home, her new life. The life that might not happen.

Mom heaved the roast from the oven and wrestled it onto their oval Christmas platter. Hadley took the rest of the potatoes from the oven. Both of them were going through the motions.

Leanne poked her head in the door. "Everything all right in here?" She rested a hand on her bulging stomach.

"Almost ready to serve," her mother said briskly. "Would you please get out the carving set and put it at your father's place?"

"You bet. Just give a holler if you want me to help you bring the serving plates out."

"Got it covered," Hadley said. Was Leanne beginning to waddle? She wasn't due for four months. "Go back in that room and calm down those Indians."

After her conversation with Brock, she wondered if this whole group might be a little too much for him. Two years ago, he'd found her family "authentic," a "real American brood." Now they were chaotic.

"Would you bring out the roast, Hadley? We can get started." Mom pushed the plaid headband back in her hair. Hoisting up her grandmother's large oval platter trimmed with gold, Hadley carried it into the dining room.

Dad stood at the head of the table, knife in hand, with Aunt Ethel next to him. Her mother's aunt always came for Sunday dinner. Even though she didn't have kids, the children never seemed to bother her. She always showed up with some game that endangered Mom's Murano glass collection. Today it was a golf pitch station. Every time it clicked, her mother twitched.

When Hadley bustled back into the kitchen for the green bean casserole, her mother handed her the Christmas Pyrex dish. "What about Aunt Ethel?"

"What about her?"

"She's going on that cruise. Why don't you ask if you can go along?"

"Are you kidding? I could never do that." This green bean casserole was hot.

"Why not? She's mentioned taking you more than once, but you've never had time. This could be your chance. Your aunt can be a lot of fun."

"But isn't it too late?"

"So what? She has a suite. Probably plenty of room." Mom did look wistful. Maybe she wanted to leave the hot kitchen and the clamoring children behind. This could be tempting.

Giving her a guilty look, Mom began to fool with the curls at the back of her neck. "Your father would never allow me to go."

"Of course not. Who'd do the cooking?" Hadley set the Pyrex dish on the counter. "Isn't it kind of cold for a cruise?"

"This is a Christmas market cruise. Sounds ideal to me. Shop your brains out. You know my aunt. Nothing but the best when it came to travel."

"Yes, well Uncle Oscar spoiled her." But he'd been gone for a while.

Her great aunt had always been generous to Hadley. When she became engaged, Aunt Ethel promptly gave her a set of white

Limoges china. Sent it over by courier. "I have no one else to leave it to, my dear," she'd said when Hadley called to thank her. "My entertaining days are over. Use it with your friends and have fun."

"Margie?" Her father called out from the dining room.

"Better get going. Just thought I'd put a bug in your ear." Mom pushed through the swinging door. Hadley picked up the casserole and followed her.

"Let's all take our seats." Brandishing his knife, Dad began to carve.

"Kevin, when are you going to learn how to do that?" Mindy asked as they watched the neat pink slices fold over onto the platter. Hadley didn't think she could eat a thing.

Kevin gave his wife a strange look. "Why would I want to do that when my dad does such a good job?"

"Every man should know how to carve a good roast," her mother twittered. "Leanne, start those beans and mashed potatoes around, dear, would you please?"

"I don't see it." Kevin dug in his heels. "And I don't have a good carving set."

"Christmas is coming," Leanne threw in. Did that mean that Steve was getting a carving set for Christmas? Probably.

In the middle of this carving discussion, one of Kevin's boys began to wail. "I don't like mashed potatoes. They're so white." Jackson was the middle child and was always trying to get attention, or so Hadley thought.

Aunt Ethel took another sip of her manhattan. "If we didn't eat anything white, we would never have ice cream either, would we?"

"A great point." Kevin gave her a pleased smile.

Jackson folded his arms across his chest. "And none of that goopy gravy either."

The silver gravy boat was making the rounds and Hadley's mother looked more than a little offended.

"I guess you don't want dessert then?" Mindy asked.

"Let's stop the nonsense. Pass your plates." Her dad motioned with the knife. "I'll serve you." He always said that with a sense of accomplishment.

So the plates came and went. The green beans were followed by the mashed potatoes, with the gravy boat right behind. But today, Hadley sided with Jackson. She absolutely did not want gravy. Her stomach felt upset. Mom's suggestion had her thinking. Getting out of town would solve a lot of problems. But how could she broach this with Aunt Ethel?

"Two slices or one, Hadley?" her father asked. All she really wanted was a half slice but she held up one finger.

"How are the preparations coming for your Christmas cruise?" Mom asked Aunt Ethel. Hadley couldn't even look up. This was way too obvious for her.

"Oh, wonderful. I've been reading up on those wonderful cities and their Christmas customs. You know, mulled wine and flakey pastries." Her aunt had a real sweet tooth. Their bonding moments often happened over chocolate decadence cake or lemon bars.

"Where are you going again, Ethel?" Dad had trouble keeping all this straight. Hadley began to cut her beef into ever smaller pieces. Keeping her head down and pretending to eat might get her through this meal.

"We begin in Amsterdam, then cruise down the Danube." Her aunt was practically singing now and Hadley stifled a giggle.

"The Danube. Oh, I can hear that waltz now." Mom looked Hadley's way. She wanted to disappear under the table.

"Then on to Cologne, over to Prague, Vienna. Budapest for New Year's Eve." The cities all sounded grand. Hadley had been hoping to plan a wonderful honeymoon, but Brock was more a Caribbean than a Danube guy.

"Such romantic cities," Aunt Ethel told Mom over the green beans. "Why, when your Uncle Oscar and I went, he bought me the most gorgeous set of pearls in Vienna." Uncle Oscar had an eye for jewelry and had given his wife some stunning pieces before his somewhat early demise in his sixties.

Glancing down at her diamond, Hadley felt her stomach lurch. Taking the ring off would mean it was over, and too much was at stake. She was going to think things over. Brock would come around. Dropping her hands into her lap, she covered her ring finger with her right hand.

But her aunt was staring at her. "I'm sure that handsome young man of yours will book a trip for you after you're married."

"Have you finished your Christmas shopping, Aunt Ethel?" Mom asked in a blatant attempt to change the subject.

Aunt Ethel poured a liberal amount of gravy over her roast beef. This was a woman who didn't know her cholesterol count and didn't care. "Heavens no," she sputtered. "I just write checks. I'm not about to endanger myself in those Christmas crowds.

Good heavens, the malls are probably full of pickpockets waiting for elderly people like me who look like vulnerable targets."

Dad looked over his glasses at her. "Now, Ethel, if there's one thing you are not, it's a vulnerable target. Your purse alone could take out the fifth Battalion."

While they all chuckled, Aunt Ethel sniffed. "I do so like my handbags, even though my doctor thinks they've given me shoulder problems."

"I told you I do not want any potatoes," Jackson was at it again. Poor Mindy looked beside herself. When Mom wasn't looking, Mindy scooped up Jackson's plate. Taking her knife, she scraped the mashed potatoes onto her own plate.

Hadley's brother didn't say anything. Wasn't this how all families worked?

"And eat your green beans, Noah," Mindy said, digging into those mashed potatoes. "Your hair will fall out if you don't."

Noah wrinkled his nose. "That's not true. Look at Grandpa. He always eats his beans."

Poor Dad. The top of his head looked so shiny under their chandelier. The comment had the table roaring. The atmosphere had changed and Hadley began to relax.

"Are you bringing Brock here for Christmas Eve or Christmas Day, Hadley?" Leanne asked innocently.

The question jerked Hadley's head around. "Are we ready for cake?"

"Not yet, dear," her mother said.

The conversation moved on and Hadley settled back. For a

while, they talked about the kids' Christmas plays and the upcoming Christmas break. Lots of plans had to be made. There were Christmas cookies to bake and movies to see. Then the conversation briefly circled back to their aunt's trip, which did sound marvelous.

Finally it was time for dessert. Jumping up, Hadley helped clear the table with Leanne and Mindy. After Hadley brought out the chocolate mousse cake, her mother sliced off generous pieces. The Christmas conversations ebbed and flowed around her. She could hardly wait to escape to her quiet condo.

When everyone was sitting back, too stuffed for a second helping of cake, her mother suggested coffee in the living room. Great. But everyone continued to sit there. Finally, Hadley escaped to the living room with her mug of decaf. The last thing she wanted was to be up all night. Sleep had been elusive since Brock had given her the news of their "break."

She discovered Aunt Ethel sitting in front of the Christmas tree. Now, her family's Christmas tree always looked as if it was going right through the ceiling. Her mother had a thing about a full tree. It never occurred to Mom that to have a full tree, it had to be really tall. And they only had an eight-foot ceiling.

"Wasn't that a great meal?" Hadley slipped into the chair next to Aunt Ethel. Sometimes she felt her aunt got overlooked. The children always managed to steal the spotlight.

"Your mother's a wonderful cook." Her aunt turned to her. "You're kind of quiet tonight, Hadley." Aunt Ethel had always had a keen eye. Over the years, they'd developed a close connection.

"Brock and I are taking a break," she whispered.

"A break?" Aunt Ethel looked as clueless about this as her mother had been.

"Yes, we're kind of assessing things, you know." She couldn't admit that Brock had decided he didn't want children. In this family that would be very hard to explain.

Aunt Ethel's brows lifted into her gray hair. "So Brock wants to take a break. Is that what I'm hearing? That doesn't sound very jolly for you, my dear."

"Oh, well, it's just one Christmas." She tried to laugh it off.

Her great aunt wasn't laughing. "The Christmas of your engagement? I'd say that's a very special time."

"Yes, well, Brock's busy. You know how that goes."

But Uncle Oscar had probably never asked for a break from his wife.

"Would you like to take a trip?"

"What? Oh, I don't have time. And I've spent so much on the wedding."

"Nonsense. This is a gift. An all expense paid vacation. You'd be helping me really."

Hadley's eyes teared up. Her aunt always said the sweetest things. Had Mom spoken to her? How humiliating.

"Please, dear. I'd be so pleased if you joined me. The suite is large. And you'll see Christmas markets in several cities. Get to know their customs. Think of it as an education."

Her great aunt bent her head closer. "It would be the best Christmas gift you could give me. Two weeks. Please come."

Noise erupted in the dining room. The last thing Hadley wanted was to sit here for Christmas, answering questions about Brock. Jackson appeared in the doorway with more chocolate mousse on his face than he had in his tummy.

"If you're serious, Aunt Ethel, I would love to come."

Chapter 2

Jurgen heard his little girl before he saw her. Clara's voice echoed down the carpeted hallway. "I hate Miss Schmidt. Hate her! And she will not get any Christmas presents from me!"

Turning from his suitcase as his daughter rocketed through the doorway, Jurgen felt his jaw clench. "You must apologize at once for saying that. What if Miss Schmidt heard you?"

Standing before him, she linked her little fingers together. As usual, Clara didn't look at all contrite. Her face was smudged, her hair was wild and where had she gotten those clothes? "Can I apologize to you and not her?"

"Miss Schmidt is not 'her.' I have told you that before. She is Miss Schmidt, a nanny who loves you very much." But that might not be the case if his daughter continued with this behavior.

"But Miss Schmidt does *not* love me. When she brushes my hair, she always pulls it, Papa."

His little girl was mashing her right foot into the deep carpet. Right now he didn't have time for this tantrum. "Have you packed for the cruise?"

Clara's eyes drifted to Jurgen's leather luggage that sat open around the room. Emerson had been working on them all morning.

"No. And that is why I hate Miss Schmidt."

Going over to one of the high-backed chairs in front of the marble fireplace, Jurgen sank into the soft leather. This chair had once belonged to his father, King of Starengard. The leather still retained the faint scent of his father's pipe. Somehow he found that comforting, especially when he was at odds with Clara—which happened frequently.

Her long blonde hair probably should be cut but he didn't have the heart. That hair reminded him so much of his wife, now gone. Her bright blue eyes stared at him, more steel than the blue of a sunny day. Clara's torn shirt and slacks would have to be thrown away.

"Let me guess. You have argued with Miss Schmidt about your wardrobe. Again."

Dropping her eyes, Clara nodded. "I'm sorry, Papa. But I do not want to look like Miss Schmidt."

She had a point and he struggled not to laugh. The matronly governess was hardly a fashion plate. Jurgen brought his long legs up to the hassock. Clara was not sorry at all. In any case, Myra Schmidt was right. It was time that his seven-year-old began to dress like a girl. Like a princess. The thought made him smile. Right now she looked like anything but royalty.

"Why don't we compromise…" he began.

"Papa," she said with a sigh far older than her age. How could his seven-year-old daughter act like four sometimes and then thirty-four another? She would age him before his time. Jurgen rubbed his tired eyes.

Meanwhile, Clara threw herself up onto his bed. "Come-prize? Does that word mean I get a prize?"

He had to laugh. And that was the problem. When he should be disciplining the princess, he was laughing. "No. Compromise does not mean that you get a prize. You are too spoiled as it is."

"No. I'm not." She lifted that delicately turned up nose so like her mother's. It was Christmas. This year he wanted to be happy. For her sake and for his. Was that Shatzi barking somewhere?

"Well, I could argue that point, Clara, but I don't think I will." The yapping in the hall grew louder.

Clara's dachshund Shatzi careened into the bedroom to create even more delightful confusion. Emerson had mentioned that the dog was to be groomed that morning. Obviously she'd escaped.

"Here, Shatzi. Come here!" Getting up on her knees, Clara beckoned to the dog. Needing no further encouragement, Shatzi scrambled up the small wooden staircase kept next to the bed and settled next to his mistress.

Poor Miss Schmidt came plodding along to stand in the doorway. Her gray hair was pulled tight into a bun and her ample bosom heaved. Whether it was modesty or just an inability to appreciate fashion, Miss Schmidt wore her dresses long. And her sensible shoes with ties had never been in style. He'd be horrified if Clara grew up to favor that type of shoe. Liesel's heels with the red soles had been so high that she often had to cling to his arm at official events. He'd teased her about it.

Those shoes and gowns. He did not have the heart to get rid of them. No, they still were stored away in her closet. And he was the only one with the key.

"My apologies...Your Royal...Highness."

He always held his breath when Miss Schmidt attempted to curtsy.

"No need for an apology. I have just been working with your charge, hoping we would have her ready for the dancing on New Year's Eve. You know, on board the ship." That was a stretch but Jurgen believed in establishing goals.

"Dancing?" And with that Clara was on her feet. Shatzi joined her, barking and leaping about on her short little legs. "But I don't want to dance, Papa. I want to fly!"

When her arms stretched out as if she might leap from the bed, Jurgen jumped up to gather her into his arms. "Now, now, Clara. We cannot have another broken leg. Not for Christmas. Santa does not come to little girls with broken legs."

For certain he would have coal in his Christmas stocking this year. But navigating the ship with a little girl on crutches would be difficult. And not at all the carefree holiday he'd pictured.

From behind lowered lashes, Clara studied her papa. The minx knew all too well how to twist him around her little fingers. She made his heart ache and fill with joy at the same time. "Maybe we can come-prize, Papa." She stumbled over the word.

Jurgen set her down. "When it comes to flying, there will be no compromise. The only flying we are doing is when pilot Gunther flies us to Amsterdam to board the ship next weekend."

Clara looked up at him. And it was a long way to look. She was small for her age, although Liesel had been strong and hearty—well, before her illness.

"What will you give me if I am a good little girl on the cruise?"

The outrageous demand made him laugh. She should be thrilled to be going on a cruise like this. The Christmas markets were sure to be a delight, although Clara insisted she hated to shop. Most fathers would be pleased with that. But all Jurgen wanted was for his daughter to be a little girl that liked to dance and wear ruffled dresses. Her ballet lessons had lasted for two sessions. And his mother was complaining about her behavior.

"I think you will have more than enough reason to be a good little girl on the cruise. Remember that Santa Claus is coming. And he only comes to little girls who behave."

"We are having some trouble with her wardrobe..." Miss Schmidt began.

"And that is a familiar problem, isn't it?" Going to one of the long narrow windows, he turned to send Clara a stern look. But she had dropped to the floor to wrestle with Shatzi. Even the dog ignored him. Shatzi was probably waiting for one of those biscuits kept in a bronze container up on the mantle. Right now, he could hardly see even a hint of bronze under all the holly leaves and pine boughs.

Miss Schmidt drew closer. "Princess Clara wants to only bring…" Here she leaned forward to whisper with great horror. "…pants."

"Well, I won't hear of it. What about the formal dinners in the evenings?"

"But I don't like to eat dinners at night," Clara wailed. "I eat only peanut butter and jelly and cinnamon toast. You know that, Papa."

Although he heard Miss Schmidt's intake of breath, he did not acknowledge it. "You will not be allowed to eat at the table unless you eat from the menu the chef has prepared." That was a tall order. One that he regretted as soon as he'd said it.

Looking perfectly happy, Clara folded her arms. She often mimicked him, but he would not laugh. He could never tell if it was intentional. "Fine. Miss Schmidt and I will eat peanut butter in the room."

Miss Schmidt's disappointment was evident. "You can choose from the menu," he assured the nanny under his breath. "Even if you do end up in the room."

"And also, she wants to bring the dog."

Here he drew the line. "Shatzi will not be coming with us, Clara. We are taking a vacation. Hannah and the other servants will be happy to watch her. These plans have already been made."

"But without Shatzi, I will be very lonely." Clara pulled a very sad face. She was good at that.

"Oh, but my little sweetheart, you will have me. Your papa. And you will have Miss Schmidt."

By this point, Clara had stretched out on the floor with Shatzi besides her. Hooking one leg over the other she began to kick the hassock. But Jurgen wasn't giving in on this. His mother, the Queen, complained constantly that Clara lacked good manners. This trip would be a chance to train his only child away from the disapproving eyes of her grandmother.

He clapped his hands. "And now go and get ready for lunch. And Miss Schmidt, please send Emerson in."

Jumping up, Clara followed her nanny out the door. The second they reached the corridor, Shatzi took off after her. What a relief to be without all that barking for two weeks.

"Yes, your Highness?" Emerson appeared at the door, shaking his head and chuckling. He got quite a kick out of Clara. But when he saw Jurgen, the smile quickly faded.

"Emerson, I wanted to make one point as you finish up the packing. Remember, no one is to know who we are. We are simply a widower and his daughter traveling for the holiday."

"Of course. But you will be occupying the Royal Suite, correct?" Emerson's forehead wrinkled. The man did try so hard. How old would he be now? Maybe seventies? Jurgen didn't have the heart to retire the man, who had also served his father. Emerson did so well with all the details and was an excellent resource for protocols. Maybe on this trip, they would have a chance to sit down and talk about Emerson's future.

"Correct. But you did allow a passenger to occupy the other half of that third level, correct? We will not occupy the entire floor. That would be too obvious." Thank goodness his mother would not be traveling with them this winter. She had other plans, or so she said. Privately, Jurgen felt she could not face two weeks with Clara in such close quarters.

"Yes, Your Highness. They have upgraded one party. Without children, as suggested."

"Perfect. And tell Captain Holthausen absolutely no recognition. We may simply sit at his table at times as guests."

"Yes of course, Your Highness. None whatsoever. At this point even he is not aware that you will be on the ship."

"Wonderful." How he looked forward to being a normal person, whatever that might be, for just two weeks. Without Liesel, the holidays had become very difficult. After three years without her, Jurgen wondered if life would ever be normal for him again.

Chapter 3

Maybe taking this cruise with Aunt Ethel was a mistake. Brock was all Hadley could think about as she got ready to leave. She probably should stay home and try to work on their relationship. Brock might have a change of mind. Shouldn't she be in town in case that happened? But after she'd agreed to accompany Aunt Ethel, there was no way to turn back. Her mother assured her of that. "Aunt Ethel is so excited, sweetheart. You two will have a wonderful time together."

"I think you're just relieved that you won't have to worry about me."

"Nonsense. I'm sure Brock will come to his senses, dear," Mom had told her during one of the final phone calls. "Keep in touch."

"I'll be posting on Facebook."

"Oh, that. You know I don't use it."

"But Leanne does." Clearly her mother was preoccupied with her holiday preparations. She always went overboard, and Hadley felt excluded this year. It was as if her mother thought she'd taken care of Hadley's crisis by sending her off. Last week Hadley sat down with Miranda, her assistant, to give her detailed instructions. After working together for three years, Hadley had complete faith in Miranda. She would be able to handle any calls that came in. The holidays were always a slow time anyway.

Aunt Ethel was being so sweet about everything. She'd even booked a limousine to take them to the airport. They'd gotten their connection in New York and now here they were, about to board the ship in Amsterdam.

"Isn't it beautiful?" Aunt Ethel gazed up at the ship while a porter took their luggage from a cab. Hadley had been delighted that the ship was relatively small, accommodating only about three hundred people. *Take that, Brock.*

But this wasn't his kind of cruise anyway and she wasn't here to think about her fiancé. In a moment of weakness, Hadley had sent him a Christmas card with a note that she would be "evaluating their options over the holiday." That sounded so impersonal. But in her heart, she knew what it meant. The family option versus the successful professionals option.

She could approach this like a business proposal. Line up the benefits versus the drawbacks so she could neutralize the negatives. That's exactly how she approached marketing a problematic property. She'd list the pros and cons to identify and bring out the most favorable outcome. Against her better judgment she'd closed her Christmas card with "Hope to see you when I return."

So far, she hadn't heard anything from him. Not even an email. She supposed he'd be with his parents in Winnetka for the holidays. Playing tennis with his father at the club. Enjoying his mother's catered dinners. But she would not think about Brock now. She kept his ring on her finger. As far as Hadley was concerned, they were still engaged.

And what was not to like about this dream vacation? Aunt Ethel had taken care of every little detail. Good thing because Hadley had been so busy closing the deal on South Shore Enterprises, an apartment building being converted to business condos along the lakeshore. Despite that pressure, she'd done a little shopping before packing up for the trip. A winter white outfit had been a bit of a splurge and so was the red cape. Still, she'd earned it, hadn't she?

"The men will take care of all of our luggage," Aunt Ethel told her after they'd been directed to the ramp. "Just look at that splendid Christmas tree inside the doorway."

Hadley held the collar of her red cape snug around her neck as she boarded the ship. Why hadn't it occurred to her that this Christmas cruise was going to be cold? Maybe Brock was right. A Caribbean cruise would be better during this time of year.

Hadley followed her aunt into the reception area, where classical Christmas music played in the background. Waiting next to the most beautiful tree she'd ever seen, the staff all wore black or red jackets and broad smiles. The atmosphere was upbeat and her spirits rose.

"Mrs. Romerly and Ms. Parker." The woman at the desk read from her list and began talking to Aunt Ethel while Hadley took it all in. The tree rose two floors, flanked by split staircases. Red poinsettias lined the steps and giant glass ornaments were suspended above them. All these green, gold and red decorations would decorate her parents' house four times over.

Smelling of cloves and cardamom, a plate of beautifully frosted Christmas cookies sat on the counter. She was tempted but Brock's words echoed in her ears. They'd been at Casey Rivers' party after the Bears played the Buccaneers when he turned to whisper, "It takes a lot of self control to be as slim as Gisele Bunchen." Well yes, the model was stunningly slender when the video cameras picked her up cheering for her husband in their private box. Sucking in her stomach, Hadley turned to study the Christmas tree.

"Ready to go to our room?" Aunt Ethel asked after talking at length to the woman in a low tone that Hadley couldn't overhear.

"What floor are we on?" she asked, starting toward the staircase. These steps would be a great workout for her thighs.

But her aunt was headed in another direction. "Oh no, dear. We'll take the elevator at the end of this hall. I believe we're on the third floor."

"Really, but I thought…" Trotting along behind her aunt, she nodded to people and smiled. After all, they'd be with this group for two weeks and thank goodness no one knew her. She was away from home. Away from pitying eyes. If she had stayed in Chicago, her family would have felt sorry for her. Hadley hated to be pitied.

Her feet sank into the carpet as they marched along. "This carpet is really top shelf, isn't it?" She was impressed.

"If you're going to cruise, cruise in style. At least that's what Oscar always said." Aunt Ethel was practically singing and Hadley smiled. Her aunt was such a kick.

Marching down the hall, they passed some open doorways giving glimpses of vacationers getting settled. The air crackled with excitement. Was that Bing Crosby singing "White Christmas" over the sound system? The Christmas spirit stole into her heart and Hadley was determined to keep it there.

Finally, they reached the elevator. Aunt Ethel pushed a button and the burnished wooden doors slid open. They stepped inside. A distinctive scent of Christmas spice filled the air. Closing her eyes, Hadley could dream of Christmas with all the holiday trappings. How she wished she'd given in to the urge to sample just one cookie at the desk. But no way. Widening her stance, she straightened her shoulders. If she were ten pounds thinner, would things have gone better with Brock? Maybe.

The elevator doors opened with a whoosh and they stepped out. Except for some stylish pillars and two elegant settees, the long hallway was totally empty with impressive double doors on either end. "But where are the rooms?" Hadley asked. "I think we're on the wrong floor, Aunt Ethel."

"Oh no, dear. We're right where we should be." Looking at the keycard in her hand, her aunt turned to the left. "I think our entrance is this way."

"Really? This doesn't look anything like the pictures I found online." She felt like Alice in Wonderland. The discreet buttons tucked here and there along the hallway probably did all kinds of wonderful things.

Her aunt walked up to a pair of double doors sporting boxwood wreaths with enormous red ribbons and waved the keycard. The doors swung open. "What in the world?" Yes, Hadley was in a completely different universe. Stupefied, she followed her aunt inside. The doors closed quietly behind them. "But this is someone's living room."

In front of her was a wall of windows giving a view of the water. She could only imagine how breathtaking this would be as they traveled. Dove gray drapes hung on either side of the windows. The room was carpeted in a slightly darker shade of gray. And the sofas were a delicious shade of turquoise, accented by silver holiday pillows. But the focal point was a Christmas tree decorated with a dizzying array of aqua and lime green ornaments. "Wow, this is really something."

She stepped closer. The ornaments were interspersed with a colorful collection of figurines that seemed to be folk art, no doubt gleaned from different countries they would visit. On a gleaming side table sat a silver bucket holding a chilled bottle of champagne.

"Lovely. They have outdone themselves." Slipping off her cashmere coat, her aunt draped it over one of the gray leather chairs.

Hadley slowly unbuttoned her red cape. "Are you sure this is our suite? Maybe someone else's name is spelled like yours. Why don't you stay here and I'll go down and talk to that woman at the desk."

Her aunt turned toward her and Hadley saw that mischievous smile. This was the smile Aunt Ethel had worn the weekend she took Hadley away for a "casual weekend in a warmer climate." They'd ended up at the Ritz in Naples, Florida, in the middle of the worst winter the Midwest had ever experienced. Her brother and sister had been green with envy. But as her aunt told her, they had their children to keep them company.

That's when Hadley noticed their luggage tucked behind one of the sofas. She would know her new jewel green bag anywhere. And her carry-on as well. She'd chosen that color so no one would mistakenly grab her luggage from the endless supply of black bags on airport carousels.

"I hope you don't mind, dear," her aunt said. "I made just a few changes to our reservation. We were so lucky because this wonderful suite had become available. Can you imagine that some poor soul came down with a nasty flu bug? Of course I'm terribly sorry for them." Here she crinkled up her nose. "I decided you and I both needed a special trip this year. Your room is to the left."

That's when Hadley noticed the double doors flung wide at either end of the suite. What looked like a king-size bed beckoned.

And that's when the Christmas craziness began.

Chapter 4

Emerson unpacked his suitcases while Jurgen checked to make sure everything in the suite was in place. Yes, even the card on the bottle of champagne said "Welcome, Mr. Lundborg." Excellent. Liesel had been the one so particular about the amenities on their cruise ships. "We should go one notch higher," she'd said. "Be one-of-a-kind."

His wife had been very smart. But now he was here for a vacation with Clara this Christmas— just the two of them. Without their full staff scurrying around, they could do anything that normal fathers and daughters did. Emerson and Miss Schmidt had rooms directly below them, close to the elevator.

Going out onto the balcony, Jurgen took a deep breath. The crisp winter air felt so bracing, so freeing after the stuffy royal quarters. His responsibilities as head of state fell away. In any case, his mother could handle anything that arose during his absence. He had thought of blocking her on his phone to ensure a pleasant vacation. But that would be rude and he would never hear the end of it. Glancing to one side, he spotted an older woman sitting out on the balcony of the other Royal Suite. Looking very peaceful, she sat there smiling. Very promising indeed if he had a quiet older couple with him on the third floor.

Back inside, he picked up the parchment sheet from the desk and scanned the activities for the coming week. Wonderful. They would stop at the cities he loved. With Clara, he'd enjoy shopping for Christmas specialties.

He'd given strict instructions to Miss Schmidt to pack Clara's prettiest sweaters and heavyweight slacks so that she would not get cold. His mother has seen to it that his little girl had pretty dresses for the holidays, if he could persuade her to wear them. Included in his list were her leather boots. No more tennis shoes for Clara. He did not want to see a single tennis shoe on this trip. Then again, he'd agreed that she could pack her own carry-on bag. "For my private things, Papa," she'd told him with an impish grin. He had no idea what was inside. And it was a sizable bag. But he would not worry about that now. She had whisked it away to her private room on the plane.

The bell rang. When Emerson stepped over and opened the door, Miss Schmidt stood there. What now? Her face redder than usual, she was wringing her hands. Alarm tightened his chest. The woman prided herself on her composure. She was not given to fits of embarrassing emotion. This did not look good.

"What is it?" They hadn't even left the dock and already they had an emergency?

"It's Clara. I can't find her anywhere." She gave up the words grudgingly, as if she hated to admit this. Good heavens, not even out of port and she'd already lost his daughter?

"Have them announce something overhead. Immediately." But

the expression on her face reminded him of his anonymity. "Yes, we can't do that, can we? But you've got to find her immediately."

"But Your Royal Highness…"

"No, no, no…" he had to cut her off or she would be calling him that for the next two weeks.

"… Herr Lundborg," she began again, shaking her head, as if she couldn't understand why they were bothering with the charade. "I was giving her a tour and she just disappeared. I can't imagine where she went."

"What floor were you on?" He began to pace, his boots sinking into the carpet.

"The first floor."

"Emerson!" His workout would have to wait. Would she have slipped out past the entrance? Had she seen something on the shore and gone chasing after it? "Please enlist Emerson's help. She must be on the ship."

Emerson came rushing from the bedroom area. "We have an emergency," Jurgen told him. "Please help Miss Schmidt find Clara. Check the children's area. Didn't we have an activity and area for children put in on each ship?"

"Yes, top deck." Emerson was on it.

But Miss Schmidt was already shaking her head. Clara would never seek out designated space for children. Play with other kids who followed the rules? That wasn't her style. Jurgen was both proud and exasperated by his daughter's independent temperament. "Just find her."

Emerson was already moving toward the door.

***

Ah, here it was. The laundry room. Backpack in hand, Hadley pushed open the door. Thank goodness, the room was empty. Now all she had to do was figure out how to use one of these washing machines. Closing on the South Shore deal had taken up most of her time and energy this past week. Sure, she'd done a little shopping. But she'd had no time to wash her favorite ripped jeans, workout shirts and a few other personal items. Heaping them onto the counter, she studied the instructions on the machine. They weren't simple.

Any idiot could do this, right? Letting a wave of exhaustion come over her, she rested her forehead against the cool metal. This morning it had been so hard to stay perky with Aunt Ethel. She was being so kind about this trip and Hadley didn't want to appear ungrateful. Their suite was wonderful. Aunt Ethel might take any bad mood personally.

With the door closed and no one else around, she let the full weight of her situation wash over her. Although she'd never surfed, Hadley imagined this was how people felt as they were swept under. How could this have happened with Brock? Everything had seemed so right. They would be the perfect, upwardly mobile couple. How could she have been so blind? So insensitive, if she took Brock's word for it. She'd never discussed the children issue with him, or so he said. Sniffling, she patted her pockets for a tissue. Nothing

What was that? A rustling came from behind a closed door at the other end of the room. She sniffed and straightened. Hadley hoped they didn't have mice or, even worse, rats on the ship.

She looked around. Grabbing a broom propped in a corner, Hadley inched forward. The noise continued and she hesitated. Maybe she shouldn't try to handle this. Was there an emergency phone somewhere? She could call for the staff. Just as she was trying to decide, the door slowly creaked open. A little girl with long blonde hair stuck her head out, and Hadley expelled a sigh of relief. The girl's eyes widened and she looked as though she might shut that door again.

"Well, hello there." Hadley smiled and set the broom aside.

"Hello." The little girl was dressed in a fashionable line of corduroy slacks but her top was on inside out. On her feet were black leather boots. Could those be real leather on a child her age? "What's going on in there?"

With that, the little girl yanked the door closed behind her and leaned against it. "Nothing." Her accent was charming and Hadley wondered what country she was from.

"Are you looking for your parents?"

The girl shook her head.

Hadley eyed the gleaming row of six machines. "Washing your clothes?"

Biting her bottom lip, the girl's eyes circled between the machines and Hadley. Good heavens, she was being sized up by this little thing, who now nodded seriously. "Yes, I most certainly am."

Most certainly? "How old are you, if I may ask?"

"You may." When the tyke gave her nose a curious imperious

tilt, Hadley held back a laugh. "Seven." Okay, she was small for seven. Hadley's nephew Stewart was seven but he was much taller than this kid. More muscular too.

"My name is Hadley. What's yours?"

"C-Clara," she said with some hesitation.

Hadley smiled. "Like the little girl in *The Nutcracker*?"

"Yes, we have many nutcrackers at home," she said seriously. Her arms did a wide sweep. "All over. You know, for Christmas."

With that, Hadley began to laugh. This kid really was a trip. "No, I meant, the ballet."

Clara frowned and moved away, inching toward the door. "I hate ballet and I'm not going to another lesson. Not ever."

"Oh, okay." Why did Hadley feel that a line had been drawn? The girl wrenched the door open and disappeared. Well, she didn't know what to think about that. Dumping her clothes into the washing machine, Hadley grabbed a packet of soap from the counter, opened it and poured soap crystals into a slot. Then she closed the door and set the controls as best she could. Time to go work out.

No way was she going to ignore her exercise routine while she was on this cruise. *Ten more pounds.* That was her goal. Brock would have second thoughts about this "break" when he saw her.

After Aunt Ethel had given her the name of the cruise line, she'd gone online to make sure that the ship had a workout room. And it did, on the first floor. As an extra bonus, a track ran around the entire second floor, so she could run too. She'd discovered a staircase that went up to the top deck and down to the other floors.

Taking the stairs might be faster than the elevator. Now she walked down to the end of the corridor and entered the door marked Fitness Center.

Excellent, no one was here. The equipment all seemed to be top notch and the place was so quiet. Hopping onto a treadmill, she punched in her settings, watched the angle rise slowly and then chose the outdoor track on the screen. Then she popped in her earbuds and pressed her playlist. She'd changed her default to Christmas songs just before she left.

Twenty minutes later, she was working up a good sweat when a guy jumped on the treadmill next to her. A little annoyed, she hoped he wouldn't try to make conversation. They were the only ones in the place. A few flicks of his fingers and his treadmill picked up speed. Lean but muscular, he must be a runner. He'd plugged his earbuds into their system so he was familiar with the equipment. Looking very serious, he took off.

Time for a change and Hadley switched her video setting to the beach walk. Gulls flitted through the sky on the screen in front of her. If she closed her eyes, she could feel the cool, flat sand beneath her feet. Waves lapped the shore. Yes, she was on some Caribbean beach. With Brock. The way they had been during their last Caribbean cruise. Hand in hand in the warm sun. She was really getting into this. Arms pumping at her sides, she imagined how great this would be. Had she just groaned?

The touch on her elbow startled her. Hadley's eyes flew open. Dripping with sweat, her neighbor was frowning at her. What the heck? Losing her pace, she began to slide. *Oh no oh no oh no.* Soon she'd be pitched off the end onto her… A large hand slammed the red emergency button on her machine. Thank goodness. She grabbed the handrails to steady herself. "Thank you."

"Never close your eyes on a treadmill," he was saying as she popped out her earbuds. "It is a very dangerous thing you are doing."

Her gratitude took a nosedive. What right did he have to tell her what to do? She'd have to change the time she worked out if this creep would be here. Granted, without the workout towel around his neck and skin shiny with perspiration, he could have been an ad for men's cologne. Yeah, maybe he could replace Matthew McConaughey.

But she didn't like his condescending attitude. Pressing the button to return the treadmill to the lowest level, she struggled to rein in her irritation.

"Especially when you have it set at an angle."

Would he ever shut up? Hadley pushed the Off button. "That's my thigh tilt," she told him, totally irritated. Did everyone on this cruise ship have an accent? Well, it was an international cruise.

"Thigh tilt?" He looked totally baffled. Hopping off the machine, she left. So much for seasonal Fa-La-Lah on this ship.

Chapter 5

When she dressed for dinner that night, Hadley pulled out some of her new purchases. Why not start the trip on a good note—especially after being lectured to by that rude guy in the fitness center. After she dressed in her winter white sweater and slacks, she swept her hair up into a high ponytail. Working with her hair, she couldn't help thinking of that little girl. How could her mom let her out with that messy hair and her clothes turned inside out? And what was she doing in the laundry room without her mother?

"You look stunning, darling," Aunt Ethel told her as they met in the main room. The privacy of the suite was wonderful. Her aunt had a spacious bedroom and bath at one end of this salon while Hadley had her own on the other end. They couldn't even hear each other running a shower. She did a little twirl.

"Winter white." Aunt Ethel's eyes shone. "Could anything be more elegant?"

"The sweater feels so soft. I love it." She really didn't need the Monet shawl. But the brilliant water lily scene added a nice splash of color and she arranged it over one shoulder.

Checking the mirror over the marble fireplace, Aunt Ethel fingered the pearls that shone against her red knit dress and she primped her waved hair. "What do you think of this color, dear? Be honest now." Before they'd left Chicago, she'd had her hair done in a new color. Hadley loved that about Aunt Ethel. She was still a woman who took chances.

"I think that reddish auburn is fabulous."

"Thank you. I thought so too." And with that, Aunt Ethel picked up her black file clutch and followed Hadley out the door. The door clicked shut behind them.

Waiting for the elevator to arrive, Hadley felt a sudden rush of affection. "Thank you for bringing me on this wonderful trip."

"My pleasure. I am so glad to have you with me, sweetheart." Her aunt squeezed Hadley's hand. The elevator door opened and they stepped inside.

"Is this elevator private?" Hadley studied the rich wooden panels. "No one else seems to use it."

"I believe so. Just the guests in the other third floor suite and us."

The doors swooshed open on the second floor, which held the main dining room. Staff stood waiting and Christmas music sparked in the air. A smiling maître d' in a black tux escorted them to their table. Tonight, everyone had assigned seats—at least it seemed like that. Dressed in a navy military jacket, a man who sure looked like the captain stood as they approached.

Hadley had to admit there was something very appealing about a man in uniform. This man's jacket held colorful bars and symbols trimmed in gold, along with the logo of the cruise line. His hair shone like pewter in the low light. "Good evening, ladies. I'm

Captain Holthausen. May I?"

As he held out their chairs, Hadley decided this trip held promise. Well, except for the fitness center. But she wasn't going to think about that now. Already seated at the table was a couple about Hadley's age, maybe a little older. They introduced themselves as Eva and Frederick Basel. "Our honeymooners," the captain said.

Hadley felt the smile freeze on her face. She couldn't even look at Aunt Ethel. But her dear aunt leapt into the gap. "A honeymoon," she trilled. "How lovely at Christmastime. What made you choose a Christmas market cruise?"

As Eva talked, Hadley had to look away from the happiness radiating from the new bride's face. How she wanted to be that girl. But she wasn't. Snapping open her napkin, she made an effort to join in the conversation. Thank goodness, they could choose their seating for meals. After this, she'd have a heart-to-heart with her aunt about circulating to other tables.

Champagne was poured and they had just been served the appetizer course when a man slid into the empty chair next to her. Hadley's hand froze as it lifted her champagne flute. The guy from the workout room. Really? After taking a sip, she gave him a reserved nod. No need to indicate that they'd met earlier. But her aunt greeted him as if he were her long lost nephew.

The bubbles tickled Hadley's nose. She began to sneeze but somehow got it under control while the others introduced themselves. Hopefully, she wasn't going to be running into this man a lot. His name was Jurgen something-or-other.

Snapping open his white linen napkin, the newcomer said, "Ladies, you're looking elegant tonight."

Had Aunt Ethel noticed Hadley's hesitation? She'd explain later. His trim navy sport coat emphasized broad shoulders. She wondered how much weight he pressed and how often he worked out. She intended to avoid him or he might be lecturing her the entire cruise.

Her chilled asparagus and polenta was topped with a poached egg and loads of Parmesan cheese. "This must have hundreds of calories," she murmured. Her hands went to her thighs.

"You could use a little weight, dear," her aunt murmured in an undertone.

"Right." One trick she'd learned was to cut everything into tiny bites. The food then took longer to eat. The others were digging right in. Jurgen was wolfing it down with crisp, decisive bites and so was the captain.

"This is the first real food I've had since we left New York," her aunt murmured. Nothing wrong with her appetite. Hadley pushed the cheese and the polenta aside, nibbling at the asparagus.

When the waitress came to clear the table, Jurgen glanced over. "Was the appetizer not to your liking?"

The waitress had stepped back.

"I have a very…small appetite."

Aunt Ethel raised her brows. Hadley nodded up at the waitress, who then took her plate. Would this man continue to question her behavior? But to her relief, the conversation turned to the cities they would visit. Hadley was proud of her aunt, who knew quite a bit about their destinations. Frederick and Eva seemed to be holding hands under the table. He looked at his wife with such adoration that Hadley had to pull her attention away. The main entrees were served.

"Is everyone going on the shore excursion tomorrow?" Jurgen asked as he sliced into his steak.

The couple nodded. "Of course," Aunt Ethel said. "We can hardly wait to see the Christmas markets."

Since she'd never been to Amsterdam, Hadley was eager to explore. "Will there be many markets?"

"Oh yes." And Eva began to describe them. The Basels lived in the Netherlands so they had been on this cruise before.

As she nibbled at her salmon, Hadley was grateful for the extra lettuce on the plate. It was easy to hide chunks of fish under the green leaves. But at one point she caught Jurgen frowning at her in obvious disapproval and she blushed. "I had a lot to eat today," she murmured, although that was a total lie. She hated plane food, even in first class.

But how irritating. Who did he think he was? First he criticized her for closing her eyes on the treadmill, when she had everything under control. And now he was overseeing her eating habits? Granted, Brock had that base covered but they were engaged. Glancing down, she flexed her fingers and her beautiful diamond responded to the light. Well, she thought she was still engaged. This was only a break. Right? Looking up she caught Jurgen studying the ring and she buried her hand in her lap.

Turning her attention to her aunt, she listened to her talk about the wonders of Amsterdam with the captain. Jurgen and the Basels joined in about the places they'd visited in the city. The art museums seemed to be the couple's main interest, while her aunt loved the flower market. "All those tulip bulbs."

Dinner moved at a leisurely pace. Would it be like this every night? It had been a long day and Hadley's eyes felt heavy. Maybe she shouldn't have had that chardonnay after the champagne. But her aunt was enjoying the lively conversation. Then it was time for dessert.

"No chocolate mousse for me," she told the waitress, but not until the woman had deposited a charming dessert pot patterned with gold leaf in front of her. The chocolate looked rich and deep. She could almost taste it on her tongue. *This is hopeless.*

"No mousse?" Jurgen picked up his spoon. She wished he'd mind his own business.

Across the table, Frederick began to feed Eva little spoonfuls, while she looked at her new husband with adoring eyes. Hadley definitely had to explore other seating arrangements.

"You realize," Jurgen began in that accent that some women might find charming, "that this mousse is infused with chile. That extra…" He waved one hand, flashing some sort of signet ring while he searched for the right word. No doubt Jurgen had attended some exclusive European university. Men and their class rings.

"Tang," Aunt Ethel supplied, as she carved out a spoonful of that super chocolaty dessert topped with a generous dollop of whipped cream. She turned to Hadley. "Sweetheart, I'd offer to eat yours but I just can't."

"The mousse is very good. Excellent, in fact. The kitchen must use a high grade of chocolate." More useless information was thrown out as Jurgen savored his mousse, while the others continued eating quietly.

By that time Eva had called a halt. Maybe that was how she kept that super svelte figure in her lovely green knit dress. When Hadley looked down, she'd already swallowed half of the mousse. And yes, that chile was a big hit with her taste buds. Hadley could feel it teasing the back of her tongue. If only she didn't like chocolate so much.

"Wasn't that tasty?" Jurgen was relentless. He clearly was not interested in healthy eating. Would she have to justify her choices this entire cruise?

But oh, that mousse sure was delicious. And the flavoring was unique. She didn't want the kitchen to think that she wasn't appreciative. Picking up her spoon, Hadley finished it off.

Coffee was served, but Aunt Ethel seemed to be nodding off. "Ready to leave soon?" she whispered to Hadley, folding her white linen napkin. "I'm falling asleep."

"Yes. Of course." What a relief. They said polite goodbyes. The gentlemen stood and nodded. There was something about the way Jurgen held those broad shoulders that was almost military.

When they reached the elevator, Hadley turned to her aunt. "I'm going up to change and then I have to check my laundry."

"You could simply leave any laundry out for the staff to pick up. There should be a bag in your bathroom."

Now that was a bit over the top. No way was the help on the ship seeing her most personal items. And her designer jeans with the slits needed special handling. She'd dashed back down once before dinner to switch everything to the dryer. "Shouldn't take long."

"All right, dear." Aunt Ethel stifled a polite yawn. This had been a big day for her. The limo had picked Hadley up at the break of dawn that morning. When they got back to the suite, Hadley dashed to her room and switched to jeans and a sweatshirt.

Then she scurried out and down the stairway that took her to the first floor. When she reached the laundry, the room was empty. The automatic lights flickered on when she came through the door. Although most of her things were dry, the ripped jeans were not. Taking out everything but the jeans, she set the dial for twenty more minutes. Then she wandered over to the bulletin board and began reading the notices. The list of excursions for the week was impressive. She wanted to do everything and she knew her aunt had already made some choices.

The dryer hadn't been going that long when she thought she heard a dog barking somewhere. Going out into the hall, she glanced in either direction but saw no dog. Probably her imagination. Did they even allow pets on this ship? Back to the excursions. She was just reading about a trip to see some windmills when the sound came again. And yes, it was a pathetic little yelp.

Going to the door where Clara had exited earlier, Hadley slowly opened it. A little brown dog threw itself against her ankles. "Oh my goodness." She sank to her knees and the dog began madly licking her chin. "You poor thing. What are you doing in here?"

Someone had come in behind her and Hadley turned. "That's my dog," Clara said taking the poor thing from her arms. Then the little girl backed away, as if she thought Hadley might steal the dog. Obviously the dog knew her. That little tail was wagging wildly.

"What's he doing in that room?" Opening the door, Hadley glanced inside. Lined with shelving, this looked like a broom closet for supplies. A large bath towel was curled on the floor next to two bowls: one with water and the other holding food pellets. Was this a stowaway?

"She's a girl and I brought Shatzi with me."

"Shatzi? How darling." Reaching out, Hadley stroked the dachshund's silky head. "But why don't you take her to your room?"

Clara regarded Hadley with serious blue eyes. "Because Papa would throw her in the river."

"What? How awful."

The little girl gave a solemn nod. Her poor little heart was probably breaking.

"Can't you have the dog in your room?" There were probably rules about that.

"Then Papa would see her. He said no. That he would do away with dear Shatzi."

Hadley had to think this over. "Shatzi. What does that mean?"

"Sweetheart. She is my sweetheart." Right now, Clara's sweetheart was squirming from her arms.

"Have you fed her?"

Her little shoulders came up. "I left food in her bowl." She opened the door and together they peered inside. Indeed it seemed that Shatzi had eaten some of the pellets. Back in the corner were pet pads that Hadley had seen advertised and the dog had used those.

"What can I do?" Clara said. "If I take her to my room before the boat leaves, Papa will throw her in the river or send her home. And there is no one to care for her there."

The story had changed and a red flag went up in Hadley's mind. She leaned back against the shelving. This tale was outrageous and she felt suspicious. But something was obviously wrong. The dog must be in some danger or she would not be here in the laundry room. If someone heard Shatzi bark, they might report the dog. Then where would Clara be?

"So you need someone to keep her just until dinner tomorrow?" Wasn't that when they were going to haul up anchor and head down the river?

"Yes and I will give you… a prize."

"A prize?" She almost chuckled but Clara was a kid who could cut you with a look. She liked to be taken seriously. These details were sketchy but for some reason Hadley didn't want this little girl to lose her dog. And she didn't want the dog penned up here. Her large bathroom came to mind.

The dryer had stopped humming. Taking out her clean jeans, she spread them on the folding counter. "I have a large room." Hadley couldn't believe she was saying this. "I might be able to keep Shatzi until tomorrow night."

"Oh, thank you. Thank you so much." Grabbing Hadley's legs, Clara buried her head between her knees. The girl's knotted hair felt soft when Hadley patted her head.

"You're welcome. But only for one night."

"One night. Yes." Stepping back, Clara disappeared into that back room. When she reappeared with Shatzi on her leash, she also carried a basket of supplies. Her eyes fell to Hadley's ripped jeans.

"Oh, you are poor," the little girl said with a sad shake of her head. "I'm so sorry."

"What?" Hadley glanced down. Surely these ripped jeans had reached the continent, but maybe not in children's sizes. "No, I'm not poor. These designer jeans are in fashion and quite expensive in the United States."

"Girls wear these in the United States?" Clara looked skeptical. "Torn clothes?"

Hadley laughed. "Yes. So don't worry. I will take good care of Shatzi." Folding up her jeans, she tucked them in the basket on top of the dog supplies and added her other clothes.

Swooping down, Clara gathered her dog in her arms and kissed Shatzi's head. "I will meet you here when the ship begins to move, okay? Tomorrow night."

Their plan sounded very clandestine. "Yes, do we know what time that will be?"

Clara shrugged. "I'll stay awake until I feel the engines. Then you will be here, yes?" She must cruise quite a bit.

"Yes. Don't worry." She had to reassure her.

Cracking open the door, Clara looked out. Then she made quick motions with her hands. Hadley didn't know how to decipher them and decided the kid watched too many spy movies. Heading in the opposite direction, Hadley took off.

Thank goodness the stairway was not far away. When she reached the suite, Aunt Ethel was outside on the balcony, probably taking in the city lights.

"Is that you, Hadley?" she called out.

"Yes. Be right there. I'll just put my laundry away." With that she disappeared into her own suite and closed the double doors. The bathroom was probably the best place for Shatzi. The room was far enough away from her aunt that she might not hear a tiny yip. Going into the bathroom that was larger than the living room in her condo, Hadley set down the basket. Shatzi promptly jumped out and begin sniffing around while Hadley explained some of the finer points. "Your food and water are right here. And your pads too."

Clara had done a wonderful job of organizing everything. The thought of having a father who would threaten to throw the dog overboard made Hadley so angry. She might have to plan an intervention but meanwhile the dog could stay here.

Turning on some music in the bathroom, she quietly closed her bedroom door. Then she joined her aunt on the balcony. The air was cold and she shivered. "I don't know how you can stand to sit out here."

There Aunt Ethel sat, bundled up in her winter coat with a blanket thrown over her knees. "My dear girl, I didn't come all this way to sit in the suite—as wonderful as it may be. I want to take in the city lights."

The Christmas lights from the ship were reflected in the water below and in the distance Hadley saw city lights on the horizon. She wasn't in Chicago and anticipation rippled through her. But right now she felt drained. "As beautiful as all this is, it's been one long day. I'm going to turn in now. Don't stay up too late. Sounds like we have a big day ahead tomorrow."

"Now you sound like your mother."

"I know." They laughed together and Hadley turned to go inside.

"What did you think of that gentleman at the table tonight?"

"The captain? He was very charming." With his silver hair and sparkling blue eyes, the captain was obviously doing his best to keep everyone happy.

"No, not that one. I'm talking about the dark-haired young man next to you."

Her cheeks heated. "He was in the fitness center when I was there earlier. Kind of full of himself, don't you think?" She didn't want to admit that he'd embarrassed her about closing her eyes on the treadmill. Maybe he'd been right.

"Was that your first impression of him?"

Hadley nodded. "We don't have to eat at the same table every night, do we?"

"Oh heavens, no. We can eat where we please. That's the good thing about a cruise. You meet a lot of people."

"Good. See you tomorrow."

She never wanted to see that guy again. But this was a small ship. Inside her bedroom, she set her watch to get up early so they wouldn't be in the fitness center at the same time.

Chapter 6

How did she ever end up feeding a dog? But Shatzi was so darn cute. The next morning Hadley was up early. Not only did she want to feed the dog, she felt she should reassure her too. "Don't worry, you sweet little thing. Clara loves you very much. And I'll make sure you don't…come to a bad end. I have a surprise for you later."

Rolling onto her back Shatzi offered her tummy for some loving pats. How could Hadley resist? Then she gave the dog two treats and took off to exercise. The fitness center was empty when she arrived. Thank goodness. She'd been worried about that and she shook the tension from her shoulders. After she hopped on the treadmill, she set the tilt. Thinking of the mousse from the night before, she increased the speed a little.

About a half an hour later, Hadley was dripping. Her legs felt like jelly and she was tempted to take the elevator up to her suite. *But no, no. None of that, Missy.* Instead she took the stairs two at a time, feeling the pull in her thighs. Excellent. Back in her room, she showered and talked to Shatzi who stood outside the huge shower, her little tail wagging furiously. She was adorable and every time Hadley recalled what Clara had told her, she got angry all over again. She'd turned the music up in the bathroom so she could talk to her charge while she dressed. Cocking her head to one side, Shatzi seemed to listen intently.

After slipping into her red sweater and torn jeans, Hadley tugged on her red cowboy boots. The boots had been part of her pre-cruise shopping spree. They'd caught her eye because she knew Brock would probably have hated them. Revenge shopping could be so satisfying. Turning in front of her three-way mirror, she decided the boots looked pretty hot. Festive too. After quietly closing the door to her bedroom, she tiptoed past the scrumptious tree down to Aunt Ethel's door. Leaning her head against the door, she listened. Her aunt did this quiet wheezing thing while she slept. Perfect.

Hadley had a plan. While Aunt Ethel was at breakfast, she would let Shatzi have the run of the suite. That might be risky but she felt terrible about keeping the little dog contained. Clara must miss her something terrible. But their separation would all be over tonight. She took the elevator to the second floor.

Down in the formal dining room, more than a few eyes took in her boots. Meanwhile, Hadley felt as if she'd stepped into a winter wonderland. All around her, tiny white lights winked. In the corner stood a tree, its limbs weighed down with green and gold ornaments. Gold ribbons cascaded from the huge star at the top. And wonder of wonders, somehow the room managed to smell like fresh spruce.

The breakfast bar looked more than tempting. That spread was just one thigh-expanding calorie after another, from cheese danish to eggs benedict. Dressed in their crisp white coats, all the staff were eager to help her. "And what would you like, Miss?"

Everything. But Hadley just shook her head. Their excursion today included lunch at a waffle house. No way would she eat her usual salad when she could have a genuine Belgian waffle. After all, it was Christmas. Visions of waffles and Christmas cookies danced in her head. But for right now, she would limit herself to coffee.

Holding that thought, she scampered back down the hall to the elevator and up to the room, a mug in hand. Time to take in the beautiful morning. Beyond the expansive window, the sky was a crisp winter blue. Before going out onto the balcony, she pulled on her silver quilted jacket. Then she quietly slid open the door and slipped outside, coffee in hand. Her breath was a puff of white on the morning air as she took a seat in one of the chairs. After a good night's rest, she was feeling much more positive. She was in a different country and could put her "break" from Brock behind her.

From where she sat, Hadley could make out Christmas decorations along the shoreline. Water lapped against the ship and every so often she heard voices from the balconies below and the deck above. Setting her red boots on the deck rungs, she sat back. If only Brock could see her now. Maybe she'd take a picture. Taking her phone from her pocket, she stood and turned to take a selfie against the skyline. Then she posted it. "Heading into Amsterdam today!"

Back home she never had much time to post on Facebook. From early morning until late evening, she ran from one client meeting to the next. She would check Miranda's staging of the properties and make sure that the photography for any brochures sent the right message. Speaking of messages, she checked her phone. Nothing from Miranda. That was a good thing. And nothing from Brock. Not so good. She went back inside.

Soon her aunt poked her head out of her room. As always, her makeup was impeccable and she was wearing one of her red Christmas sweaters with a beaded reindeer prancing across her chest. "Here you are, my dear. Ready for breakfast?" Her eyes fell to the coffee in Hadley's hand.

"I've already eaten. Is that all right with you?"

"Perfectly all right," her aunt assured her. "I enjoy eating with people I don't know. Another opportunity to make a new friend. That's the delight of these cruises. I'll be back shortly. The bus leaves at ten thirty so I'll watch my time." She glanced at the gold Patek Philippe watch on her wrist, a gift from Uncle Oscar one Christmas.

"Enjoy your breakfast." Hadley's hand was already on the door to her room.

As soon as the door to the suite had closed, Hadley dashed back inside to let Shatzi out. Settling onto the long sofa in the salon, she laughed as the little ball of fire cavorted around the room. She must be a perfect match for Clara, who seemed to have a lot of energy herself. After a good stretch of the legs, Shatzi leapt up on the sofa, all warm and cuddly. Putting her front paws on Hadley's chest, she licked her face.

"Oh no. You are a sweet girl but no licking, okay?" Although she loved the affection, Hadley patted the cushion beside her. After Shatzi stretched out, Hadley scratched her behind the ears. The dog settled with a pleased moan.

Stroking Shatzi's silky, short coat, Hadley realized that this was another thing that she didn't have in common with Brock. He'd drawn a line at pets. They were way too much trouble every time you went on vacation, or so he said. "You can't bring them along, of course, so you incur extra expenses." Brock's mind always seemed to convert everything into dollars. And although she admired his business mind—their drive was one thing they had in common—now she saw that it had drawbacks.

Her family had lots of pets growing up, both cats and dogs. But she could see Brock's point. A home was probably more orderly without them. The same would apply to children. But that thought left her with an empty feeling inside. Peace and quiet were a good thing. But for a lifetime? Hadley wasn't so sure.

Anyway, here she was, on a Christmas cruise with someone else's pet. Had Clara been brave or foolish to bring her dog along? Hadley might never have the details. After about half an hour, she took Shatzi back to her bedroom just in time to hear Aunt Ethel enter the suite. She turned on the music in the outer bedroom, washed her hands and went out to talk to her aunt.

Shortly after that, they went down to meet the bus. "Oh, I always love being taken to all the sites." Aunt Ethel glowed as they joined the short line. As Hadley mounted the stairs of the bus, she noticed Clara giving her a little wave from the end of the line.

"Is that little girl waving at you?" her aunt asked.

"Yep." Hadley waved back. "We became buddies in the laundry room."

"Isn't she a little young to be washing her own clothes?"

They sidestepped down the narrow aisle between the cushioned coach seats.

"She seems very precocious. Very capable," Hadley told her aunt.

"And look who she's with. My, my." Aunt Ethel craned her neck to look out the window as they took two seats together.

Staring out the window, Hadley couldn't believe it. *Are you kidding me?*

Aunt Ethel settled into the aisle seat. "Is that the good-looking man that sat next to you at dinner last night? What a cute pair they make."

"I wonder where his wife is." She pictured a blonde, like Clara.

When her aunt drew closer, Hadley caught a whiff of her Youth Dew, Aunt Ethel's signature scent. "Widowed," she whispered. "Very sad. The captain told me last night during a private moment."

"How sad." So all poor Clara had was Jurgen. Life could be cruel. All Hadley could do was shake her head. This was not the time to tell her aunt the sad story. Clara and her dad took seats at the front. The bus filled with passengers and they were off.

Christmas decorations had made a wonderland of Amsterdam. Every road was festooned with colorful lights, wreaths and garlands. While the bus whisked them from one site to another, the tour guide from the ship kept up a running commentary. People on bikes were everywhere. The art museums piqued her interest, both the Rijksmuseum and Van Gogh. "I'll bet that's where Eva and Frederick are today." Maybe someday she'd return.

"That's the way it is, my dear." Aunt Ethel patted her hand. "A cruise can be a sampling. Always so much to see. And you can always come back at a later date."

All around her, people were trying to see out the coach windows. Clara's dad had her on his lap. Obviously excited, the little girl pointed to everything. Soon they arrived at a square with a sixty-foot Christmas tree, or so the guide told them. Across from the tree was a fifteenth century royal palace. The size of the palace and the extraordinary decorations took her breath away.

"At nights the plaza is filled with carolers and musical performances," the guide said. "Because Amsterdam is the country's capital, our Christmas tree is the most important one in the Netherlands."

"Will you just look at that?" said Aunt Ethel. Together they stared at the tall tree. Then the bus pulled out and moved on. Amsterdam was a city of canals and as they drove across the connecting bridges, every canal was filled with lights. The boats parked along the shoreline seemed to have a Christmas decoration competition going on, each boat decked out for the holiday.

But as the tour guide spoke, Hadley was a bit distracted by Clara. She kept turning around to send secret smiles. When they drew up to an open air market, the tour bus stopped. "If you want to buy your Christmas gifts now," the tour guide announced, "this would be the place. But remember, we will be stopping at many

Christmas markets during the cruise. You'll have one hour here."

Although Hadley had left gifts with her mother for the family, she intended to pick up some small things for the nephews and her niece. Excitement rippled through the crowd as they filed off, many of them carrying shopping totes. Aunt Ethel's eyes sparkled. She loved to shop.

They began to walk. The stalls before them glittered and glowed, each more colorful than the next. Counters were stacked with everything from dolls to nutcrackers. The scent of cinnamon and cloves was in the air when they passed baked goods. The cookies were decorated so beautifully. "Let's pick out just a few," Aunt Ethel said, slowing her steps. "You know, for the room."

Her aunt was going to be a bad influence. "If we take them back, we'll eat them."

"Well, my dear. That's the whole idea."

The last thing they needed was more food in the room. Hadley's jeans and black stretch pants had to fit throughout the trip. After only one day on the road together, she realized that Aunt Ethel spelled vacation F-O-O-D.

As they stood at the stall selecting the cookies, Hadley thought she felt Clara's father's eyes on her. She would not look back at that terrible man who'd threatened to toss darling little Shatzi into the river. How could he?

They moved on to the next counter. "Oh, just look at the colorful mugs and plates. And the demitasse spoons. Uncle Oscar always bought them for me wherever we traveled."

Hadley had seen her aunt's spoon collection and knew how

much it meant to her. As Aunt Ethel moved on, bakery bags in hand, Hadley lingered behind. Ten minutes later, she caught up at a jewelry stall. By that point her aunt seemed to have acquired more bags. Hadley scooped them up and they moved on together.

When it became time to head back to the bus, Hadley was laden with bags and most belonged to Aunt Ethel. She'd insisted on buying things for the boys and a doll for Amber. "But this is our first stop. Remember what the guide said," Hadley warned her.

"Oh yes. I'll keep these gifts in mind. My, we have so much room in our suite to store these away." Her aunt was unstoppable.

When they reached the bus, she was dismayed to see that the only seats available were the two in front of Clara and her father. The little girl looked delighted and kept patting the back of the seat.

"Do you two know each other?" Jurgen asked as Hadley slid in and sat down, followed by Aunt Ethel.

"Oh yes, they're laundry room friends. Didn't you know?" Aunt Ethel asked brightly, turning around.

"The laundry room?" Jurgen looked puzzled. Clara dropped her eyes but not before Hadley saw the mischievous tilt of her lips. This was the time for secrets. Later Hadley would fill Aunt Ethel in on Jurgen.

The bus moved on to more historical sites, all dressed in seasonal finery. Then they pulled up at a waffle house. The smell of fresh waffles hung temptingly in the air. Hadley didn't know how anyone could walk past without stopping. Disembarking quickly, they all seemed ravenous. As they filed into the restaurant, Hadley guided her aunt to a table where there were only two seats. It wouldn't do at all to be thrown together with Clara and her father. She wanted to relax on this trip. Shatzi was still hidden in her bathroom and that angered her no end.

A waitress brought their menus. Thank goodness each entrée was accompanied by a picture. The Belgian waffles looked especially tempting. Who could resist? The strawberries on top looked fresh. All around them people were cutting into fresh waffles, topped with mountains of whipped cream.

"They're very light," her aunt told her. "Made of air. Really, I've had them before."

"I don't think my body got that message." Hadley giggled. As they sat waiting for their order, Aunt Ethel struck up a conversation with two women at the next table who had also been here before. They compared notes and cruise plans. With great effort, Hadley restrained herself from looking at Clara, sitting with her father at a window. Their waffles arrived and all conversation stopped.

The waffles were everything she'd heard about. They were light, they were tasty and they were topped with strawberries and huge dollops of whipped cream. She would never be able to duplicate these and maybe that was a good thing. Although she had the Tap it and Count app on her phone to keep track of her food choices, Hadley willed herself not to count the calories. Not today. And maybe not ever on this trip.

Over at the window, Jurgen seemed to be having a tense conversation with his daughter. Were they talking about Shatzi?

How miserable for the little girl. Clara kept shaking her head. "Whatever's going on?" Aunt Ethel followed Hadley's eyes.

"It's that awful man. He's arguing with his daughter."

"So now he's awful?" Aunt Ethel's eyebrows raised as she speared a strawberry and swirled it through the whipped cream.

"I'll fill you in later."

Aunt Ethel went back to her waffle while Hadley watched the waitress come back to Jurgen's table with what looked like peanut butter and jelly on white bread. What? Was he forcing her to eat peanut butter and jelly instead of a waffle? She'd heard of manipulating parents, but this took the cake. Hadley wanted to call the food police.

The incident almost spoiled Hadley's enjoyment of her waffle. But she'd deal with Jurgen later, although she didn't know how.

"Is something wrong?" her aunt asked, stopping with her fork poised.

"No. Not really. I guess it's none of my business." Picking up her fork, she went back to her waffle. But the sight of Clara eating a peanut butter and jelly sandwich had spoiled it for her. She tried not to look. If Brock were here, he might be splitting her waffle for her, saying that for one person to consume that many calories was almost sinful. Maybe he had a point. She looked down at her plate. Only one bite left. She scooped it up.

When they climbed back on the bus, everyone's eyes were flagging. The bus felt so warm and cozy that it was easy to fall into a food coma and nap. When the bus lurched to a stop back at the ship, Hadley woke up. But as she was exiting the bus with their bags in her hands, Clara came close enough to whisper, "As soon as the ship starts, okay?"

Hadley nodded. The kid would make an excellent undercover spy. By tonight, she would be very glad to transfer Shatzi back to her owner.

When they reached their state room, Aunt Ethel disappeared to take a nap. Perfect timing. Hadley closed the door to her room and turned on the music, but not loud enough to bother Aunt Ethel. These rooms seemed to be thoroughly soundproofed with very thick walls and, of course, thick carpet.

As the afternoon waned and evening approached, the engines started. She could feel the light rumble below her feet and smiled. The whistle blew and the gorgeous ship pulled away from the dock.

Scrawling a note to her aunt, she left it on the leather-topped desk in the main room. Then, with that enormous basket in her arms, she ducked out of the suite and made her way down to the laundry room, where Clara was waiting.

"My sweet Shatzi," the little girl crooned as soon as Hadley entered the room. "Have you been a good girl?"

"Yes, of course," Hadley lied. There had been one or two accidents in the bathroom but nothing too drastic. It was certainly worth it to save the life of that darling dog.

She sat against the wall next to Clara while Shatzi ran back and forth, her red ball in her mouth.

"Did you do any shopping today?" she asked Clara as she helped her get Shatzi back into the basket.

The little girl gave a stern shake to her head. "I don't shop. Papa shops." What an amazing family. But with no mother, things were probably different for Clara. Hadley's heart squeezed when she remembered her mother taking her to the Walnut Room at Macy's before Christmas. Having lunch under the tree that soared two floors had been their yearly tradition. She hated to think that Clara might be missing special times like that.

While she sat there wondering, Clara threw her arms around Hadley and gave her a tight hug. "Thank you so much. You saved Shatzi!"

Such a drama queen. "Will she be safe with you now?" She almost hated to ask.

"Oh yes." She nodded seriously. "Papa will not be able to send her home now."

No mention was made of tossing Shatzi into the Danube. Had Clara made all that up? Hadley wanted to ask her about the peanut butter and jelly. She wanted to tell her how sorry she was that the little girl couldn't taste those delicious waffles. But the day had been long and she was too tired.

Hugging Clara, Hadley drank in the smell of baby shampoo and dog. Unlike *some people*, those smells didn't disgust her at all.

Chapter 7

The sun cast a warm glow through the heavy draperies when Jurgen awoke the next morning. Flipping onto his back, he rubbed his eyes. What crazy dreams he'd had. Shatzi was barking. He could swear he'd heard that excited little yip she gave when she wanted attention. Was he feeling guilty about not letting Clara bring her?

Clara seemed to be holding up pretty well, but soon she'd miss her little friend. A father should be firm. He was proud of himself for handling the Shatzi issue so well. Wasn't he here to enforce strict discipline, the type expected of a crown princess? A few successes like this and he would be well on his way to producing the perfect princess he'd promised his mother.

Folding his arms behind his head he stared up at the recessed ceiling. This trip was off to a good start. He was pleased that Clara seemed to have forged some sort of relationship with that girl from the fitness center. An older mentor might be just what she needed.

But he really wasn't sure about Hadley. Was she the *right* feminine presence? She'd had a bit of whipped cream on her nose as she ate her waffle yesterday. That type of thing would not go over well at the castle. Still, she'd looked like a little girl herself sitting there with her aunt. And those red cowboy boots? Clara could not stop talking about them.

Jurgen could not stop thinking about them.

The barking came again. And this time the sound definitely was not in his head. Throwing aside the bedclothes, Jurgen pulled on a dressing gown and marched out of the bedroom. His head throbbed with anger. Yes, the barking was coming from his daughter's room. The morning sunlight flooded the salon and ornaments on the tree quivered as he stormed past to throw open Clara's bedroom doors. "What is going on?"

Her eyes wide, Clara looked lost in that enormous bed. For a moment, even Shatzi was still. From the mussed covers, it looked as if Clara had been playing that game they like to play. She would move her hands around under the cover like a mole until the dog nipped her fingers. She was so good at playing with the dog—better than playing with children her own age. But then again, the dog was tiny too, like his daughter.

"Papa? Please don't be mad." Clara looked at him with those huge blue eyes so like her mother's. But he couldn't become distracted now.

"How did this happen?" he asked, striding from one end of the room to the other. He hadn't heard the dog yesterday. How could he have missed this? "Does Miss Schmidt know about this?"

Looking miserable now, his daughter shook her head. "No."

"Then tell me how." He was ready to take off someone's head.

"Papa, Shatzi was going to be so lonely at home." Clara's lower lip trembled.

Lonely. He didn't ever want to be responsible for causing

loneliness. Halting his stride, he took a seat on the end of the bed and tried to control his breathing. Shatzi crept closer and licked his wrist. He petted her head absentmindedly. "I don't think the dog would have been lonely with twenty people around to take care of her. No, I think it is my little girl who might be lonely, correct?"

Seeing an opening as only Clara could, she nodded and climbed onto his lap. She was warm and cuddly as he wrapped his arms around her. If only he could transfer her hurt to himself. He never wanted her to feel fear or loneliness. "Two weeks is a very long time, Papa," she began in a shaky voice that grew more certain with each word. "Shatzi could never be without me for that long. She would be very sad."

Smoothing back his daughter's long, snarled locks, he nodded. Maybe he was not meant to be the father of a little girl. She was his only child and because of that, the kingdom had great expectations. "Yes, I suppose so. But you will have to keep the dog very quiet. If the others hear her barking, they might go to the captain. The ship does not allow pets, as you well know. We have to think of other people."

By that time Shatzi had decided to join them, wiggling in next to Clara. "Yes, Papa. Whatever you say."

He couldn't help but smile at that. "Right. As if you ever follow my directives." What would he do with her? But Jurgen fought back his desperation. A crown prince could never be seen as weak.

When he heard the main door open, he dropped a kiss on Clara's head. "Miss Schmidt is here to get you ready for the day. Then we can go down and eat breakfast."

"Cinnamon toast. All I want is cinnamon toast." His daughter had a way of saying that in a rather threatening tone. The scene yesterday was not one he wanted to repeat. In the restaurant, she had refused to eat until he asked for peanut butter and jelly. Then he had to send the sandwich back until they removed the crusts. How humiliating. The scene made it difficult for him to enjoy his waffles, which happened to be one of his favorites.

"Wait until you see the breakfast buffet." He liked to throw out enticing comments. But she was already scrambling from the bed.

"And Papa?"

"Yes." He turned while Miss Schmidt stood in the doorway, looking at Shatzi in horror. Obviously, the nanny had no idea that the dog had come along. And that situation had to change. He did not want his daughter to outwit all of them. "What is it, Clara?"

"For Christmas, I would like a pair of red cowboy boots."

"Red cowboy boots!" Miss Schmidt sputtered.

"I'm not sure that Santa has time to find red cowboy boots for you." Where in heaven's name would his staff find them? His mother would be horrified if Clara returned wearing red cowboy boots.

"Then have the elves get busy." And she gave him one of her knowing smiles. They'd had a long talk about Santa recently. Jurgen didn't know what she believed. At what age did children move on? Or was it to their advantage to remain believers?

"Please have Clara ready for breakfast in twenty minutes," he told Miss Schmidt before he left the room. Then he looked down. "Are those tennis shoes under your bed?"

Miss Schmidt came to join him as Clara moved to block their view. "Just a couple pair. Hadley wears tennis shoes. They're good for working out."

I give up. "Please, Miss Schmidt. Twenty minutes."

When they reached the dining room, the holiday buffet that he had approved himself some months ago was spread out invitingly. Early birds were making their way down the line. Omelets were cooked to order. Cut fruit was heaped on platters next to bowls of whipped cream studded with cherries. The buffet held bacon and sausage, poached eggs and scrambled, potatoes cooked three different ways. Breakfast trifle stood layered in crystal bowls. And everywhere artificial holly was interspersed, the red berries a glossy contrast to the green leaves. The tree in the corner had been carefully decorated with ornaments from the various countries served by the cruise line.

His heart lifted. Joining this cruise had been a good idea. Maybe this coming year would be different. Better. Happier.

Although he'd never been sold on the buffet idea—after all, in the castle, his butler brought his breakfast from the silver salvers along the massive sideboard—this morning he found it quaint and Christmasy. Wasn't he experiencing the holiday differently this year? Yes, he was the common man—whatever that was. Feeling good about this trip, he adjusted the green velvet morning jacket he wore over the white mock turtleneck Emerson had laid out for him this morning. Then he took two plates. He had no idea how parents handled more than one child. But at one time, he had wanted a large family. That had been Liesel's expectation before her illness.

He had to shut his mind off when it came to those memories.

As they worked their way down the buffet, Clara would not be tempted. No, she was going to limit herself to that blasted cinnamon toast. Had he made a mistake by asking Emerson to make sure the toast was provided? Maybe Clara would make another choice if the toast was not available. But he couldn't risk it. Once Clara had gone on a hunger strike. He could not take that chance. Besides, it was Christmas. At the end of the buffet table sat a tray with cinnamon toast. "Almost gone," the server told him. "It's been very popular." Jurgen took three pieces.

When he turned to find a table, he saw Hadley. This time she was alone and Clara went running toward her. "Oh, good. Hadley, can we sit with you?" Of course she did not wait for a reply. "No" was a word Clara was not used to hearing. Instead, his little girl plopped down next to the girl who worked out with her eyes closed.

Approaching, he did not know what to say. "Clara, we do not intrude on people's breakfast." Then he glanced down. Hadley was eating oatmeal topped with brown sugar, berries and walnuts. "How…healthy."

"Breakfast should be the biggest meal of the day. Please join me." But she wasn't smiling. The invitation had been extended grudgingly and he knew it. But there was Clara, delighted to see her new friend. And his daughter did not make friends easily. Jurgen took the chair across from Hadley, while Clara studied her new friend's bowl. Staring. His daughter was staring, although she'd been warned many times.

"You sure got a lot of food," Clara said.

"Clara, it isn't polite to comment on other people's food choices," he said softly.

"I don't mind it." Hadley pointed to Clara's plate. "Is that cinnamon toast?"

"Yes," Clara said as Jurgen finished cutting the cinnamon toast into triangles. "I love cinnamon toast."

"Me too." Hadley's eyes sparkled. "My mother used to give it to me when I had a sick stomach."

At that moment Jurgen was taking a sip of coffee and he choked, knowing what might come next.

"My mom used to do that too." But Clara's voice echoed with sadness and Hadley's smile weakened.

"Then we were lucky, weren't we?" Brightening, Hadley seemed to understand what had happened. "I mean, to have that wonderful memory."

Like magic, Clara perked up. "Lucky. Papa tells me that all the time."

Putting down his coffee mug, Jurgen noticed Hadley's hesitation. For a second she opened her lips, very full lips. He only noticed because they were wet with coffee. But then thankfully, she did not ask any questions. The painful questions. The kind that still hurt.

"So, what are your plans for today?" he asked Hadley, scooping up some eggs.

Sucking in a deep breath, Hadley said, "First I'm going to take a brisk walk around the track."

"Oh. Me too." Clara's face lit up. "Maybe Shatzi will come with me." But as soon as the words were out, Clara looked from Hadley to Jurgen. What was going on?

"Did I tell you that I have a dog?" Clara whispered to Hadley. "I am not supposed to tell anyone."

Jurgen didn't miss the twinkle in Hadley's eyes. "No, you did not tell me. What is your dog's name?"

"Shatzi. And she loves to walk." She batted her eyes up at Hadley. Looking from one to the other, Jurgen went on high alert. Something about the stilted exchange aroused his suspicion. His daughter was excellent at playing on other people's sympathies. He didn't know how, but somehow Clara had involved Hadley in hiding the dog.

"And then we're taking the excursion to Cologne this afternoon," Hadley continued.

"So are we." He would not think about the dog now. Cologne was one of his favorite destinations. "Beautiful city. I look forward to it."

Clara clapped her hands, now coated with cinnamon sugar. "Oh good. We can go together."

Struggling with mixed feelings, Jurgen handed Clara his napkin. He did not want her to become a burden. He was well aware that Clara's constant chatter could be exhausting. But Hadley seemed charmed by his daughter. By that time Clara had moved on with the conversation, sprinkling questions as she went. By the time Jurgen finished his eggs, he knew that Hadley was a realtor in

Chicago. She sold "big buildings." He had been to that city once. Very large, very busy. A place where you could get lost, with a train on stilts that rattled around the downtown area. Very different from the cozy towns and hamlets where he lived. Finally, breakfast ended.

"Be sure you check out the top deck," Jurgen told Hadley as they stood up to leave. "There are some games up there for children and adults."

"Top deck? What floor would that be?'

"Above the suites on three," Jurgen said and then wanted to bite his tongue. "You can reach it by the staircase." He couldn't very well tell her the elevator. That might blow his cover. She might realize that he was staying in the Royal Suite. Next to Hadley and her aunt.

Chapter 8

About thirty minutes later, Hadley was hitting a pretty good stride on the track that circled the second floor. What a great idea. The thick foam covering on the track cushioned her footsteps and prevented slipping as it ran along behind pockets of deck chairs. The running could keep her in shape and might also stop her from thinking. No word from Brock. Had he opened her last email, saying that she'd arrived safely? Did he care?

She had to stop obsessing. Popping her earbuds into her ears, she clicked on her Christmas playlist. The voices of Bing Crosby and Nat King Cole soothed her, bringing back happy childhood memories. The day was beautiful as the ship slowly glided along, passing homes and some moored houseboats. The trees on the decks of the houseboats made her chuckle. You would never see that along the Chicago River. But then again, had she ever stopped to look?

Yes indeed, it was Christmas and she was going to enjoy it. Hadley was humming along to "Have Yourself a Merry Little Christmas" when she felt the tug on her track jacket. She slowed down and turned. There was Clara, smiling up at her.

"Hold up," the little girl said, stumbling in her pink tennis shoes that hadn't been laced.

Although Hadley wanted to get in a good run, this little tyke was totally irresistible. "Where's Shatzi?" Hadley asked, bending over.

Clara pressed a finger to her lips. "Papa says we're not supposed to talk about her."

"Is your father still threatening to throw her off the ship?" The more she got to know Jurgen and his little girl, the less likely that option seemed. But she hadn't sorted through all that.

Dropping her eyes, Clara gave a stiff shake of her head. "No, but we can't let anybody know that we have a dog. They're not allowed."

"I see. Let's sit down." Hadley motioned to a bench and Clara climbed on next to her. "It's dangerous to walk around without tying your shoes. You might trip and fall."

Clara's little face folded. "But I see kids with their shoes like this all the time. Big kids."

"That might be. But it's dangerous. Where is Miss Schmidt?" By that time she understood that the nanny was supposed to be with this little girl at all times. How Clara gave her the slip was not a mystery.

"She does not like to walk. So she is sitting down somewhere."

"I see." After tying both shoes, Hadley got up and Clara slipped from the bench. For a while they walked together. Hadley couldn't resist singing along to the music. ""'It's beginning to look a lot like Christmas…"

Giggling, Clara didn't seem to know those words. Pressing a

button on her phone, Hadley switched to "Jingle Bells" and slipped an earpod into Clara's ear." Together they walked to the rhythm of, "Jingle bells, jingle bells, jingle all the way."

"Maybe I will buy some bells at the Christmas market," Clara told her when the song had ended.

"Great idea. Will they be a gift for someone?"

"Yes, I think so."

"Anyone in mind?" She could see Clara's mind turning.

"Miss Schmidt. I think she could use some jingle bells."

Hadley nodded. "I think so too."

They walked together for at least another fifteen minutes. Although Hadley would have preferred to jog, she enjoyed talking to Clara so she slowed her pace. On one of their passes, they discovered Miss Schmidt sitting on one of the deck chairs near a door. She must have been waiting for them to come around the track.

"Lunch time," she told Clara standing up and tugging at her long, very serviceable looking dress. Over the dress, she wore a warm wool loden jacket.

Coming to a halt, Clara brought her hands to her hips. "But I'm not hungry."

Oh, this would not go over well. "Clara did eat not long ago," she told Miss Schmidt.

"Your Papa says to come for lunch or else." The frustrated nanny was not giving up.

What was the "for else?" Clara looked from Hadley to Miss Schmidt and then meekly took her hand. "Oh, all right. See you later, Hadley."

"Yes. Later." Hadley watched them walk away. The pair hadn't gone far when the child wrenched her hand away. So much tension simmered between those two. Couldn't Jurgen do better than this? He must be the owner of a large company if he could afford a companion for his little girl. Couldn't he hire someone more suitable?

After Clara left, Hadley took up her jogging again for a couple of loops and then went up to the suite for a shower. These bathrooms were too much. She'd never seen so much white marble in one room. The restrooms in the commercial properties she sold were very serviceable, but not elegant. This counter stretched forever and of course had two sinks. The bath products were luxury quality, their labels stamped in black and gold foil. Scooping up a shower gel, along with shampoo and conditioner, she stepped into the shower and turned the dual-level water on full blast. Now this was luxury. The type she could never afford. Or could she?

That thought fascinated her. She could never have imagined being in this upper income bracket. Long hours and hard work had led her there. That was one thing she had in common with Brock. They were both driven. A very competent couple. Together, they had decided what type house they could buy in Glen Ellyn near his parents. The house payment they'd estimated was based on both their salaries.

Their house would have everything. Two offices, of course. An expansive kitchen that looked over one of the two decks in the yard with a pool. A media room would be outfitted with leather recliners for football games, since Brock was a huge Bears fan. The master bedroom would have a fireplace for those cold Midwest winters. A huge dressing room for each of them. And the bedrooms?

Only three. Now she understood the three bedrooms Brock had insisted on. In addition to the master bedroom, the house would have two guestrooms. He'd probably always known there would be no children, not in his life. Busy with her work, she'd never asked.

But she was here now and she didn't want to think about what she'd left behind. Brock would never agree to "blowing money"—that's how he would phrase it—on a trip like this. Squeezing a generous amount of shampoo into her palm, she lathered her long hair. The scent of gardenias filled the shower. Closing her eyes, Hadley felt the warm water course over her. Her tense muscles loosened and her wet hair streamed down her back.

Yep, this shower was a lot better than sitting in a therapist's office. And she'd done plenty of that in the past year. Between her work and Brock, she'd had her hands full. Her friends told her that every relationship was worth working out.

Squirting the conditioner into her hand, she applied it. Oh, wasn't this wonderful? She would be eternally grateful to her aunt for making this cruise possible. Her siblings might be a little jealous, but they had their children and lots of activities at Christmas time.

Although she knew that her aunt was perfectly capable of developing her own relationships on the ship, Hadley didn't like to send her down to lunch alone. Twenty minutes later they were in the more casual restaurant in the back of the ship, that was open to the elements. They ordered cucumber and tuna sandwiches for a light lunch.

Hadley watched the time on her phone so they wouldn't miss the bus. Her aunt had been right. It was wonderful to be taken to all the sites while a trained guide gave them information. At home in her work, she was always the one coming up with ideas. The property tours. The marketing activities that would attract possible buyers. Of course, Miranda handled all the details. Hadley wouldn't know what to do without her.

But here? She could enjoy touring. Would she miss walking hand in hand with Brock through the markets? Not really. He might hate that. On a winter cruise, he would probably spend all his time in the fitness center. And wasn't that a gloomy thought?

"Should we go back to the room?" she asked her aunt when they'd finished lunch.

"Yes, I want to freshen up my makeup." Opening her compact, Aunt Ethel frowned at her lips. "Look at these lines between my lips and my nose. Disgusting." She closed her compact with a snap. "Always use enough moisturizer on your lips, Hadley. Personally, I use eye cream. Better for these delicate tissues."

Then she laughed at herself. "Foolish to be so vain at my age, right?"

"Not at all." Aunt Ethel was very attractive for a woman her age, probably because she stayed active. As Hadley's mother had told her, when her aunt ran out of solutions for her own life, she gladly turned to someone else.

Chapter 9

When it was time to leave for the Cologne Christmas markets, two buses stood waiting. Hadley admired the organization of the cruise line. There was a guide for each bus, checking them in, handing them a printout of information and marshaling them up the stairs. Each guide held a tall, numbered red sign, unmistakable in a crowd. Their individual nametags were also done in red.

When they were boarding, Hadley didn't notice Clara or her father and felt somewhat relieved. But after they'd taken their seats, she saw Jurgen approaching. He careful ushered Clara onto the second coach. The black leather jacket and jeans gave him an athletic appearance and reminded her of how he'd looked on that treadmill. *Cancel, cancel.* She turned her attention to Clara. Instead of her corduroy slacks, Clara was wearing jeans too. But wait. Were her jeans torn at the knees?

"No little friend for you today?" her aunt asked.

Hadley pulled her eyes away from the other bus. "While you were eating breakfast, we walked together. Did you know that Clara brought a dog with her?" Time to be honest with her aunt. Well, sort of.

Aunt Ethel chuckled. "Really? I didn't know pets were

allowed."

"I don't think this is a little girl who follows the rules."

"Yes, and I remember another little girl just like that," she said pointedly.

Thinking back, Hadley smiled. "I remember you telling Mom that I was high spirited. More high spirited than my sister Leanne."

"Did that help your mother at the time?"

"I guess so. In time, she became more relaxed. But Jurgen? He's not that guy. He keeps trying to get Clara to do things his way."

Her aunt clucked in under her breath. "Poor man. It must be hard to be a single father. Especially at this time of year."

"Yes, I guess so."

"When I was chatting with Miss Schmidt, she mentioned that Jurgen had been widowed about three years ago or so. Very sad situation, from what she said."

Aunt Ethel could be so sly. "Has she been giving you additional inside information?"

"Miss Schmidt? Yes, the woman seems a little lost. After all, she only has Emerson to talk to."

"I don't know why Jurgen brought them anyway. What? He can't ride herd on his little girl on his own? Or do some laundry when he has to?"

"Some men have been… spoiled," her aunt said calmly. "And perhaps they have no other recourse than to be spoiled."

"And they can't change? That's sad for both of them." By that time Clara and her father had been seated on the second coach. Clara was staring out the window, watching people board. Looking over, she caught Hadley's eye and they waved to each other. Then the pleasant rumbling of the coach began and they were off.

"So what will you be shopping for today, Aunt Ethel?"

She folded her hands over her handbag as if she were preparing herself. "Let's see. Cologne is known for colorful mugs at Christmas time. We definitely need some of those. Maybe more ornaments for the tree. We can always use them next year."

"You mean our tree in the suite?"

Her aunt nodded. "Yes, it would be nice to give the tree our personal touch, don't you think?"

"Sure. And then we can use the decorations next year at home." But where would she be next year? Brock had never cared that much about a Christmas tree. His mother always hired people to put up their decorations. Hadley glanced down at her engagement ring. Still no word. No texts and no emails.

The Parker family was all about Christmas. Her mother had boxes and boxes of ornaments in the attic that she'd collected over the years. And she had at least three color schemes tucked away so each year she had to choose. But right now, Hadley felt lucky to have that one tree in their suite. "It feels good to be decorating a tree with you this year."

Her aunt turned. "Aren't you sweet? And I'm so glad you decided to come on this cruise. It's a lot more fun."

As they drew closer to the city proper, the tour director clicked on the microphone. "I would encourage you to eat by the bite as you move along," he said. "You will find the stalls offer a wide range of food. Tastier by the bite." Everyone laughed. "No really," he said again. "It is customary to eat as you wander among the stalls."

"And everything will be deep-fried and loaded with calories," Hadley murmured.

"You are much too young to be worried about calories." Her aunt patted her arm. "Indulge yourself."

"Just a habit of mine," she said thinking back. "Last Christmas Brock gave me a calorie counter."

"How romantic." Her aunt could be so droll.

"He was only looking out for me."

"I would have been insulted." Her aunt cast her a pitying glance and Hadley was sorry that she'd mentioned the calorie counter. After all, she wanted her family to like Brock. Surely they'd get back together, wouldn't they? Glancing at the skyline, she pointed to a spire. "Oh look. That must be one of the churches."

Her aunt threw her a quizzical smile. There would be no pulling the wool over Aunt Ethel's eyes. She knew Hadley was changing the subject.

The first market they visited was near the Cologne Cathedral. After the buses stopped about a block away, everyone piled out. Before long they were meandering through a maze of stalls. "Oh my, what is that wonderful smell?" Aunt Ethel sniffed and drew closer to one of the vendors selling potato pancakes. And yes, they were deep fried and stuffed with homemade applesauce. After sliding two five-inch pancakes onto a paper plate, the shopkeeper trickled warm raspberry sauce over them.

They smelled good and looked fabulous. Hadley had to get out of here but her aunt drew closer to the vendor. "Sometimes Oscar used to whip these up for us on Sunday mornings. I thought I'd never see them again."

Well, Hadley couldn't hurry her aunt along. Not when she had that wonderful memory attached to this high calorie, cardiac-arrest disaster. Slowing her steps, Hadley turned back toward the stall in the shadow of the city's iconic cathedral. "I think you should have some now, don't you?"

Since she couldn't let her aunt eat alone, she ordered two plates. Potato pancakes in hand, they continued to the next stall for some mulled rosé glühwein. The mulled wine smelled magical and warmed her after a couple of sips. They weren't the only ones standing and eating. Their guide had been right. Many of the tourists were sampling as they shopped. After they'd tossed their plates and napkins into the trash, they wandered around. Her aunt bought some brightly colored tea towels and napkins, and Hadley picked up a colorful Cologne tote to carry all the packages.

Catching up to some of the other cruise passengers, Hadley and her aunt followed them to another market filled with elves. The elves were everywhere, from the ski lifts that traveled overhead to the market's entrance.

"Isn't this fun?" her aunt said as they sauntered through the crowd.

"Yes, yes it is." Looking around, Hadley took in the seasonal color and warmth. Even though Michigan Avenue was wonderful during the Christmas season, nothing could have prepared her for this. Whipping out her phone, Hadley took a selfie with Aunt

Ethel. Later she could post it on her Facebook page.

The markets became more crowded and Hadley tried to keep her bearings so that they could get back to the bus. They weren't the only cruise ship passengers here today. Other colorful signs bobbed above groups of tourists. By the time they bumped into Jurgen and Clara, Hadley was getting nervous about finding their way back. She didn't see a tall red sign anywhere. What if the bus took off without them?

"Hadley! Aunt Ethel?" Waving like a windmill, Clara had climbed on top of a retaining wall.

"Come down from there." Jurgen set down some shopping bags and held out his arms. With no hesitation, Clara jumped into them.

As they drew closer, Jurgen was saying to Clara, "She is Mrs. Romerly to you." Now, how did he know Aunt Ethel's last name? Probably through introductions. He could be so attentive. She wondered if he worked in sales.

"I see you've been shopping." Hadley nodded to the two shopping bags.

"Yes, although this little girl told me she didn't like to shop." Hands on hips, he stared down at his daughter. "How did you rip your jeans, Clara?"

"Papa, these are the fashion. Don't you know?" the little girl said, as if her father was hopeless. Clara's eyes went to Hadley's own jeans and Jurgen's eyes followed. Did a smile hover over his lips?

"What do you have in your bags, Clara?" Hadley asked,

uncomfortable with Jurgen studying her jeans.

"Some decorations for my room."

Jurgen threw up his hands. "Right. But she hates shopping."

"Papa," Clara said with barely concealed disgust at being caught out.

"What did you buy, Hadley?" Jurgen asked.

"I'm letting my aunt do most of the buying." The four of them kept walking. When they ran into some charming Christmas mugs, her aunt had to buy them. While she was busy, Hadley moved to the next stall and did some of her own shopping. Although the last thing she wanted was another glass of wine, one of the stalls was selling some glühwein in darling little red mugs picturing elves.

"Papa, can I have one?"

Giving an almost comical shrug of his shoulders, Jurgen bought one, took a sip and then discreetly poured the rest into a planter. "For your bag." And he handed the empty mug to Clara. When he caught Hadley's eye, he gave her a helpless smile. The man was putty in the hands of his little girl, much the way her brother-in-law Steve was with Amber, her niece. This grumpy man. Who would have thought it?

"I think we should visit the Angel Market now," Jurgen said.

Where were they? Hadley glanced up at the street signs, wishing she'd brought a map. "Can we follow you? I was afraid we would get lost and the ship might leave without us."

Jurgen turned. "Trust me, the ship will not leave anyone behind. They have systems in place for cross checking."

"Have you been here before?" Hadley fell into step next to him.

He certainly seemed very knowledgeable.

"Oh yes. Many times." And then he clammed up. If he'd mentioned where he lived, then she had not heard it. But from his accent he definitely lived somewhere in Europe.

As they walked toward the Angel Christmas Market, she noticed strings of bright stars strung through the trees. "Look overhead." Aunt Ethel pointed to clusters of stars suspended in the trees.

"Angels." Clara was entranced and nearly walked right into a man drinking mulled wine. Putting his hands on her shoulders, Jurgen steered her away. The girl was a sprite. She ran, she twisted, she turned. Jurgen had a hard time keeping up with her.

Indeed, angels were everywhere, from the ornaments on Christmas trees to performers dressed as angels. Some walked through the crowds on stilts, somehow keeping their balance.

"I want to walk on stilts," Clara cried. "Then I will be tall like the other girls."

"And then you might fall." Jurgen didn't look convinced. Was he aware that Clara was somewhat small for her age?

"Ah, I smell waffles." Reaching for Hadley's silver bubble jacket, Aunt Ethel gave her a tug.

Jurgen was right behind them. "Clara, would you like a waffle?" There was such hope in his voice. But when his daughter shook her head, Hadley saw how disappointed he was.

Her aunt wasted no time in stepping up to the stall to buy two, and she handed one to Hadley.

"My aunt is force-feeding me," she said to Clara, who giggled. "Look, Clara. They are shaped like the church." The sweet smell of the powdered sugar dusting the cathedral waffles was too tempting for her. But Clara was holding out. Really? What kid didn't like waffles? But she hadn't liked the Belgian waffles in the shop in Amsterdam either.

Hadley made a show of taking a bite of the crispy wonderfulness, hoping to entice Clara. But no luck, although Jurgen seemed to live in hope. After he bought one of the waffles, he took a bite and then looked over at his daughter. But she had lost interest. Maybe there was too much else going on. So much to see and do in these markets.

A few minutes later they ran into one of the groups from the ship. They were headed for the Hohenzollern Bridge, known for "romantics in love," according to their guide. By that time, Hadley had had enough. She should have worn her tennis shoes and not these red boots that weren't comfortable on the cobblestones. She wished they were headed back to the ship. The afternoon was fading and a chill wind was in the air.

When they reached the bridge, the guide began to tell them about the 40,000 padlocks locked onto the fencing along that bridge. "If you have a lock, you can attach it now," he said. "But then you must toss the key into the Rhine River."

Turning, she saw that Aunt Ethel had tears in her eyes. "What is it?"

Sniffling, her aunt shook her head. "Oh, nothing. Just one of my sentimental moments. Oscar and I put a lock on this bridge. Long ago. My goodness, look at all the locks now. When Oscar fastened our lock, this bridge custom had just started."

Hadley was amazed by how many couples had locks tucked in their pockets. As they stood there watching, Eva and Frederick stepped up. They must have known about the custom because Frederick held a lock that they fastened to the bridge. After they kissed, he threw the key into the water, the gaslight catching the metal as it fell with a quiet splash.

Hadley had never seen anything so romantic in her life.

"I want a lock, Papa."

She didn't have to turn to know whose voice that was.

"I didn't bring a lock today, sweetheart." But she could hear the heaviness of Jurgen's voice. Hadley's heart carried its own weight but for a different reason.

Turning to her aunt, Hadley said, "Would you like to look for your lock?" Maybe finding it would cheer her up. How wonderful it would be to fasten a lock to this bridge and know that ten years later, you could visit it with your loved one. But if she had fastened the lock with Brock, would their love have lasted? After what had happened two weeks ago, she wasn't sure.

That's when she noticed the two men dressed in black. She'd seen them earlier in the day near the potato pancakes. Were they secret police? The men wore dark suits and khaki overcoats. Every once in a while, they would speak into their lapels. A chill settled over her.

"Is it time to go back?" Aunt Ethel looked to Jurgen.

"Yes. Our guide is here." He stepped toward their tour guide with such authority.

Soon the guide gathered the others and they walked together to the coach.

"Aunt Ethel, did you notice those two men in the crowd today?" Hadley asked after they got settled and she'd hoisted her aunt's bags up onto the luggage rack.

"Two men? I saw many men."

"No, these guys were different. Official. Dressed in black and wearing trench coats."

Looking tired, her aunt shook her head. "Sorry, dear. I'm afraid I didn't. I was too busy looking at the Christmas crafts and having fun." She seemed pleased by her bags of gifts that Hadley had stowed away.

Well, the implication was clear. Hadley should relax. Smiling, she thought over the day, which had been so much fun. No calls from Miranda with questions. No meetings to run to or clients who had issues with their new property. Just fun. She settled back. Fun with Clara and, yes, with Jurgen too.

On the ride back to the ship, Aunt Ethel fell asleep.

Later that evening they came down for a late dinner, although Hadley didn't think she could eat another thing. Those potato pancakes and waffles were still with her, but she wanted to keep her aunt company. For Aunt Ethel the dinner experience was a time to socialize.

Their mistake was sitting at one of the large tables. Soon Eva and Frederick arrived, along with the captain. Hadley would have to give this table arrangement some thought. Her aunt seemed to glory in the fact that they were seated with the captain. And when Jurgen arrived, well Hadley knew she had to break up this pattern.

This time she was aware that she could quietly ask the waitress not to include her in the appetizer round. Everything seemed to have bacon. But the smell was intoxicating, and she fought it while her aunt ordered. Sipping some of the sauvignon blanc, she chose a light chicken entre, while her aunt ordered the trout.

"But where is your daughter tonight?" Eva asked Jurgen when they were about halfway through dinner. "She was so cute with you today in Cologne."

Looking very distinguished in a dark navy velvet jacket, Jurgen put his fork down. "Unfortunately, Clara doesn't like to eat. Peanut butter and jelly is, well, her favorite."

Hadley could see how it pained him to admit that. Here she'd thought he was disciplining Clara in that Amsterdam waffle shop.

"But we could have peanut butter and jelly served here, if you want the little one to join us," the captain said.

Hadley could see that Jurgen was struggling. "That might be a good idea," he finally said. "She's only seven and I'd like her to learn good table manners."

"There's nothing wrong with Clara's table manners." Hadley had spoken sharply, too sharply. A faint blush warmed her cheeks and Jurgen tilted his head, studying it.

"Having children at the table is always a good idea. Although I have none," her aunt said, "I often eat with Hadley's family. And oh, what a bustling table that is."

Everyone laughed, but Aunt Ethel was right. If only Jurgen could see her nephews and niece at dinner, constantly fighting with each other over who had to eat more peas. Of course her brother and sister and their spouses squelched the chaos as soon as they could. But kids always found a way to break the rules. She knew that from personal experience

By the time they left the table, she was curious about what decision Jurgen would make about having Clara join them. And she wondered how many velvet jackets he owned.

Chapter 10

The next morning Jurgen woke up early. He enjoyed getting up when the world was still dark and he could plan his day with no interruptions. That had been his father's daily habit. Jurgen had taken to it easily from the time he was a teenager. Oh, his mother might have a tray brought to her room around nine in her own quarters. But following the lead of his father, he liked to get an early start.

So he'd set his watch to chime, although he groaned when it went off. He wanted to get out on that track before Hadley. The day before had left him restless and feeling very out of shape. Obviously, the young American took good care of herself. Well, except for that dangerous habit she had with the treadmill. Tying on his running shoes, he had to laugh at himself. How ridiculous was this? If he were acknowledged as the crown prince and owner of this cruise line, the staff would rope off the track for him until whatever time he chose.

But that would defeat his purpose on this trip. He was living as a "regular guy." And it was too soon for Jurgen to decide if he enjoyed it.

Before leaving the suite, he peeked in on Clara. She was fast asleep in her bed with Shatzi curled up next to her. He didn't approve of having a dog in the bed. But what did that matter? Leaning against the doorway, he took in the moment. This little girl wrung his heart. She could be such a handful for one so tiny.

One arm was thrown back on the pillow, while the other reached out to Shatzi. The dog raised her head and then plopped back down as soon as she saw Jurgen. Shatzi was probably better than any security detail. She would start barking when a stranger came near. Quietly, he closed the door.

Grabbing a sheet of the ship's linen stationery, he wanted to write a note for Clara. But how many times had she told him, "Papa, I cannot read what you write. You are too sloppy." And she'd giggle because wasn't that how he always described her? So he took his time and tried to print. Then he texted Miss Schmidt, saying that he was leaving the room. Was she awake? Herself an early riser, she responded immediately. He waited for her in the salon.

Once she had arrived, he slipped out into the hall and took the stairway to the second floor. So far on this trip, he'd avoided Hadley and her aunt by using the stairway. Thank goodness, they seemed to prefer the elevator. Jurgen didn't want to have to explain what he was doing in the other suite.

Out on the track a cold breeze hit his skin. He was glad he'd worn a warm-up jacket. Dropping his towel onto a bench, he did some slow stretches. Then he began to run at his usual pace. But his mind raced ahead of him. Another year was ending. Another year without his Liesel. And yes, each year it seemed a little easier.

The pressure near his heart had lifted a little. Not much, but a bit. Expanding his chest, he made himself breathe deeply, even though the cold air wasn't easy.

The trip had been a good idea and he was glad he'd come. Sure, in the beginning he thought he would keep himself busy over Christmas. That had been his main intent for every holiday since his wife's death. But after his mother had made that comment about his daughter's poor manners, he'd established another goal for the trip. This would be a type of training. And he would escape his mother for the Christmas holiday. Clara had insisted that Santa would not come if his mother had anything to say about it. She was always telling Clara how naughty she'd been.

He snorted. What was that American phrase? "The shoe was on the other foot." His little girl might be training him and not the other way around. But Eva's suggestion of bringing Clara to the dinner table was a good one. His little girl could see how it was done among adults. However, his pride was at stake. And he realized that now. He did not want anyone to know that he had a little girl who only ate peanut butter and jelly. As the crown prince of Starengard, his daughter's diet would matter. But as Clara Lundborg? Not so much.

Jurgen Lundborg. Did he look the part? Apparently so and he chuckled to himself. Although he'd asked Emerson to advise him about the small points, he soon realized the man was simply used to following orders. Asking advice cast Jurgen into a different role, one that might feel strange and unfamiliar to Emerson. His valet's father had been in service to the crown and his grandfather before him. On this trip Jurgen was trying to be just a man, a citizen of the world. But it was hard.

Just Jurgen. The first time someone had called him by his first name onboard, he felt himself freeze. In his usual setting, such an address would have been considered an insult. The person would have been quietly pulled aside. But not here.

As he got into his running rhythm, his eyes moved to the lights along the shoreline. People were getting up to enjoy their coffee and strudel. Normal lives. Easy lives. But maybe he was deluding himself. On this trip he had been looking at the others, trying to figure out where they were with their lives. The young couple? That was easy. They were beginning their adventure together. When Frederick helped Eva fasten the lock on the chain-link fence the day before, Jurgen had to look away.

But what was this? Behind him came the slap of feet. How frustrating. He had planned on being alone at this hour. He would have to tell Emerson to keep the track closed until eight o'clock in the morning. Maybe people wouldn't notice or care.

Then he had to laugh at himself. He could almost hear Emerson chastising him. "But Your Royal Highness," Emerson would say with all due respect, "wouldn't everyone wonder why it had been closed? Wouldn't you be giving away your identity with this directive?"

"Yes, Emerson. You are so right. So correct."

"Talking to yourself?" Hadley Parker breezed past.

She'd caught him by surprise. As the Crown Prince, he never wanted to be caught by surprise. Especially when he was mumbling to himself like an old man. Usually he was told everything ahead of time so that he could be at his best. Be prepared. But this was early morning. He hadn't even shaved because he hadn't expected to run into anyone. In fact, he'd chosen this hour because Hadley had walked later yesterday with Clara.

Now he picked up the pace so he would not lose her. No way would he be passed by a woman. Once he'd locked her in his sights, he moderated his speed. Yes, looking at her from the back was rather pleasant. "You should not listen to other people's conversations," he called out as he drew closer.

But he didn't want to pass her. In the early morning light, he could see her shadowy outline in her pink track suit. To his delight, she was not scarecrow thin like so many women today. No, Hadley had delightful curves. And that long ponytail of hers swung from side to side as she ran with a hypnotizing rhythm.

And that's when it happened. He tripped and fell flat on his face. "*Ach du lieber.*" To his embarrassment, he went down hard.

"Let me help you." Suddenly, Hadley was there, crouched next to him. She was gasping for breath, her face covered with a healthy sheen from the run.

"I don't need any help, thank you." Heaving himself onto his knees, he struggled to stand. His right ankle throbbed when he touched the ground. This was hopeless. "I'm fine."

"Don't be stubborn. You need help." With that she took a very firm hold on his bicep and pulled. He had to allow himself to be helped up or risk dislocating his shoulder.

"You have a very strong grip," he said begrudgingly as he

hopped over to one of the benches.

"I work out a lot." Once he was seated, she began to gently prod his ankle.

"What are you doing?" He stared at her in horror. She was touching him before asking permission.

"Estimating the extent of your injury." Something about her tone implied that he was a *dummkopf.* And he was far from stupid. Didn't his people tell him that all the time? But today, he was Jurgen Lundborg. *Get over yourself, Jurgen.*

"Nothing's broken." With that, Hadley jumped up and sat down next to him. "I would prescribe ibuprofen and rest. And you'd better wrap that ankle to keep it stable."

"Thank you, *dakter.*" Really this woman was too much. But he was strangely glad to have a quiet moment with her. The ship plowed through the water and the shore was far away. At this early hour, they seemed to be the only two people around.

"I want to thank you."

"For what?" Taking the towel from around her neck, she began to blot her face and chest. Okay, that was distracting. Her jacket was partially unzipped.

Where was he? Ah, yes. The thank you. "My daughter has taken a liking to you. And I can see that you might be good for her. Clara has had, well, a difficult time. So, thank you." There he'd said it. He had humbled himself before her.

A tiny smile curved her lips, while she kept patting herself with a towel. Wanting to be a gentleman, he looked out at the river, flowing so easily past them. But when she said nothing, the silence became troubling so he turned back to her. She was staring out at the river.

When Hadley lifted her dark eyes to his, they were flashing. "So does this mean that you will not throw poor Shatzi into the water?" Folding her arms across her chest, she regarded him with open defiance. What was this? Usually this was the point when the person would be ushered from the room by one of his aides. But he was all alone out here. Helpless. And confused.

Maybe she was a little bit crazy. "What do you mean? Of course I wouldn't throw my daughter's dog into the water. In America do people throw their dogs into the water?" This must be a very strange custom.

"No. Never." Those flashing dark eyes again. "We prize our pets. We allow our children to travel with them." Here she squirmed a bit. "Well, if it is allowed on the ships and at the resorts. Then we can bring our dogs. But not always."

He had to laugh. "So you take your dogs on trips with you but you do not throw them into the water? Only at Christmas time?" Where had this American custom come from? He was still trying to understand, although after all, this was a country that didn't even know how to play *futball* properly.

"I don't have a dog," she said quietly. "You know, to take on any trips."

He stopped laughing. Hadley had turned serious and sad. He wanted to know why. Wanted to smooth that frown from her brow and lift the shadow from her eyes. "Why don't you have a dog if you love dogs so much?" Jurgen wouldn't let her know that he suspected she'd helped Clara bring Shatzi onboard.

Suddenly, Hadley folded like a dumpling right in front of him. "The man I might marry doesn't like dogs." Staring out at the water, she shook her head as if this was the saddest thing in the world.

"You *might* marry him?" He glanced at her ring. Like a lot of things American, the stone was garishly large, probably a zircon.

She sniffled. "We're taking a break."

"But you still wear his ring." Yes, she should have that stone checked.

"This is just a break. I think." Hadley seemed uncertain.

"I don't understand. What does it mean to take a break during an engagement? You know, in your country." Possibly another strange American custom.

"We're wondering if we're meant for each other."

Such craziness. This woman was very pretty and so much fun. Yet her intended let her get on a ship with an aunt for the holidays? "Then this man—he is crazy and maybe you are *not* crazy." Had he really said that out loud?

Her eyes narrowed. "Of course I'm not crazy." She jumped up.

But she didn't run off. Instead, Hadley looked down at his throbbing ankle. "Do you need help getting to your room?"

"Not at all." He would walk there if it killed him.

"All right then." Turning on her heel, she left. The nearby door opened and closed behind her with a quiet swish.

Somehow he managed to stand, swaying as the boat moved. If there was a phone nearby, he would tell the captain to turn off the motors so that he could walk to the elevator. The steps were out of the question. But he didn't see a phone and he'd left his in the room. With Hadley now gone, he placed his hands on the wall and sidestepped toward the doorway that led to the elevator. When he turned into the hall, there she stood.

In silence the doors of the elevator opened and she got inside. Well, he couldn't wait. Her eyes widened when he joined her. There was nothing he could do about it. Slowly the elevator rose. When the light pinged and the door opened, of course she exited first. But she was silent until they both got to their doors. Facing each other across the long hallway, she said, "You are in the other suite?"

This was becoming complicated. "I am. Good day." He limped into his room.

Chapter 11

After Hadley had showered, she dressed in her torn jeans and a bulky white sweater. Then she laced up her new tennis shoes with pretty pink and green stripes along the soles. Her aunt was waiting for her in the salon so they could have breakfast together. Today Hadley might have to eat some sausage and maybe a cheese Danish. That was the least she could do to assure Aunt Ethel that she was having a good time. Her aunt seemed to equate food with enjoyment.

Smiling as they passed the staff, they took a table at the one of the windows. "Will you just look at those decorations?" Her aunt looked around with satisfaction. "Taking a trip like this is so pleasant when other people do the decorating and you can just enjoy it."

"I agree." This was not the time to admit that she rarely decorated.

A waitress poured their juice and they got up to make a quick pass through the buffet. Hadley had learned that the buffet was much quicker than ordering from the menu. Fine with her, but that long buffet was too tempting. Somehow, they both ended up bringing back two plates.

Sighing with contentment, Aunt Ethel sipped her coffee and munched on her pastry. As the ship glided down the Danube, they enjoyed the scenery. Homes sat up on the hills, decorated with a dazzling display of lights, still visible in the early dawn. "This must be spectacular at night."

"Yes. So beautiful." After finishing her scrambled eggs with basil, Hadley sliced off a tiny piece of sausage and tasted it. The salt seemed to wake up her taste buds. It had been a long time since she'd allowed herself to eat sausage. She chewed slowly.

"What should we do today?" Aunt Ethel said. "We'll be passing some castles. Lots to look at. And I think the ship will stop for some day trips over the next few days. More shopping. Could be fun."

But her aunt looked tired. No way did Hadley want to exhaust her when so much excitement lay ahead in Prague, Vienna and Budapest.

"Someone mentioned an activity area up on the top deck." Hadley had checked out the area the day before when they got back from their excursion. "Why don't we spend the day up there? The sofas and chairs look comfortable and quilts are folded nearby to snuggle up with. The children's area has some games too." They could just hang out together.

"Speaking of children." Aunt Ethel nodded toward the buffet and Hadley turned. To her surprise, Clara was pointing to food while Emerson filled the plate. "I wonder where her father is."

"Jurgen hurt himself this morning running."

"Oh dear, I hope it's not serious."

"He said it wasn't, but he was limping. Which might be why Clara is here with Emerson." She turned her attention back to her aunt. "Did you know that they are staying in the suite at the other end of the hall?"

"Really? So nice to know the neighbors." There it was again. That strange expression on her aunt's face, as if she were the cat that swallowed the canary.

"Excuse me, Aunt Ethel. I'll be right back." Hadley wanted to check this out. Was Clara actually eating more than cinnamon toast? That would make her so happy.

"Good morning, Clara and Emerson." She peered down at the full plate in Emerson's hand. "What have you got there?"

"My papa hurt his ankle," Clara said with disgust. "He always tells me to tie my shoes. But did he tie his shoes? No."

Swallowing a laugh, Hadley could only nod. The poor man had been in bad shape as he limped off the elevator that morning. Was that the story he told Clara? That he hadn't tied his shoes? Of course he wasn't going to admit to falling because he wasn't paying attention. "Be sure you choose a good breakfast for him. Those waffles look wonderful." Would any of this entice Clara? "Remember the little waffles we bought yesterday?"

"But these are not shaped like cathedrals." Clara wasn't easy to please. Was that because she was an only child? In some ways it was a shame that Jurgen and his wife had not had more children. Although Hadley had foolishly shared her own pathetic story that morning, Jurgen had said nothing about his wife. Of course that situation was very personal. Maybe he was introverted, although she doubted that.

"My aunt will think I've abandoned her. See you later," she said with a wave.

"See you later," Clara shot back. She seemed adept at picking up American phrases. For a seven-year-old who looked like a four or five-year-old, she was a quick study. But the one thing she couldn't master was proper eating. And Miss Schmidt should do a better job with that hair.

"What was she doing?" Aunt Ethel asked when Hadley returned. "I hope she's eating something substantial."

"I'm not sure. She's fixing a plate for Jurgen. You know, on account of his ankle." She tried to say that in a detached manner.

"So he runs early in the morning too?" Aunt Ethel said with that curious way she had of phrasing things when she wanted information.

"Apparently so." Hadley was not going to play this game. Her sausage was gone but she was still hungry. A tiny bit of pastry couldn't hurt. She did love ricotta cheese. "So what about it? Should we go up onto the deck and read or play cornhole?"

"Cornhole?" Aunt Ethel finished the last bite of her eggs florentine.

"You toss beanbags into these holes on a tilted board surface. Anyone can do it, although it does call for some skill." She could never win at it.

"I don't think I've ever been on a cruise where one of the activities was playing cornhole," her aunt said. "Shuffleboard, yes. Not cornhole, but I'd like to watch."

"That's one of the things I love about you." Hadley reached for the last bite of ricotta pastry. "You're always game for anything."

.

Chapter 12

When Hadley checked her email after breakfast that morning, she was excited to see something from Brock and quickly clicked it open. "Looks like you're having a good time on that cruise. Did you bring your calorie counter with you? It's snowing here. Brock."

She pushed back from the desk. Nothing about love. Nothing about missing her. He was actually talking about his weather and her calories. Turning the ring on her finger, she didn't know what to think. She'd posted some pictures of herself with their group in Cologne. Maybe he'd seen them.

Quickly, she fired off an email to her mother about their activities. Mom was probably waiting for news. But maybe not. Maybe her mother was so wrapped up in her Christmas preparations that she wasn't giving a thought to Hadley and Aunt Ethel. The next market they visited she would have to buy her mother something special for suggesting that she go on this cruise. Hadley didn't even want to think about how awful it would be sitting home in Chicago.

Feeling restless after reading Brock's email, she wandered into her spacious bathroom. The day was breezy and she was going to be outside. Her hair would be a mess. For the next ten minutes she french-braided her hair into two plaits, one on either side of her head. By the time she was finished, she could feel the braids pulling on her forehead but no matter.

Her aunt was waiting so Hadley shut down her laptop, wishing she could turn off her mind too. "Anything wrong?" her aunt asked as she came out into the salon.

"Not at all." She clicked off the tree lights. "Let's go see what's happening."

When they reached the top deck, she took a deep breath. The sky was a brilliant blue but the air was nippy. After all, it was December and snow dusted the houses and pastures they were passing. Aunt Ethel had bundled up in a sweater and her warmest coat and Hadley had pulled on her silver quilted jacket. Together they settled on the expansive sectionals where colorful Christmas pillows and blankets were within reach. Shaking out a lovely soft blue quilt scattered with a snowflake pattern, she draped it over her aunt's legs. "What's that you're reading?"

Aunt Ethel held up a book. "A history of royal families. Thought it might be a good read. I found it in the library downstairs—fascinating collection."

"What a great idea. Since we're here and everything." Hadley had brought her electronic reader. Why was it that in romances the couple always got together? Certainly not her own situation. When she thought of all those expensive gifts she had tucked away for Brock in her closet, she could cry. But most of them were going back when she got home.

Yes, she'd reached that point. Of course the items she'd had personalized could not be returned. But the rest? Brock would never see them. That decision gave her a curious sense of satisfaction. Lifting her left hand, she spread out her fingers. This ring was beginning to bother her. Maybe it was all the salt she'd been eating but it felt tight.

Taking a deep breath of the fresh air, Hadley clicked on her electronic reading device. She was sitting there reading when she felt a timid tap on her leg. Looking up, she found Clara staring down at her, wearing a cute green sweater. The yoke was ringed with small white reindeer. Her pants matched and she wore those wonderful black leather boots along with a green vest.

"My, you're looking pretty today." She smiled up at Clara. The little girl's long blonde hair was tied up in a ponytail that had the markings of Miss Schmidt's hand. A bit of a mess. The river breeze sent blonde strands flying.

Clara cast her eyes over at the activity section at the end of the deck. "Can I play any of those games?"

Tucking her reader into her tote, Hadley smiled. "Sure. Are you here alone?" That would be unusual.

Clara pointed over to where Miss Schmidt sat in a deck chair as if she'd been given a timeout at school. The woman was scowling. No way the nanny was going to give up her comfortable seat to play cornhole or darts. Clearly she was there to watch and maybe supervise. Looking at that iron gray bun at the base of her neck, Hadley figured that Miss Schmidt would never master french braids either. Hadley took Clara's hand. "Aunt Ethel, we're off to play games. Want to come?"

But her aunt was engrossed in her book. "See you later, dear," she said with a wave, never looking up. That book must be fascinating.

"Let's go check out the games," Hadley told Clara.

"Aw, I knew you would want to play with me." Clara looked delighted, skipping along beside her. Certainly she had friends at home to play with. Didn't she? Clara probably missed them.

Because it was early in the day, one of the cornhole sets was free. Soon Clara and Hadley were tossing beanbags every which way. Of course it took a bit for her to explain to Clara that the idea was to get the beanbags into the holes. "That's how you get points."

"Okay. I can do this." With a grunt, Clara lofted yet another bean bag into the air. It landed with a splat, two feet from the board.

Hadley had to do something. "I think we have to stand a little closer."

"I think so too." When Clara nodded her head so seriously, Hadley had to stifle a laugh.

They were both honing their skills when Jurgen limped up behind them. "May I join you?" He seemed to be balancing himself on his left foot because his right foot was all wrapped up. She wondered if Emerson had done that for him. Probably, but Jurgen needed a cane.

"So, who will teach me?" He stood waiting.

But before Hadley could say a thing, Clara was gathering the bean bags. "I will, Papa. It's very easy."

Handing her father three beanbags, Clara proceeded to give him directions on the game. Hadley was surprised and pleased by his patience with her. With his cheeks burnished by the wind and his hair upended, Jurgen was the very picture of the involved father. He'd caught the eye of more than one woman up on this deck. Did he date at all? She would think he would have no trouble in that area. When Eva arrived to take the chair next to her husband, Hadley waved at them. They looked so happy together, and she had to look away.

Pulling a chair over to lean on, Jurgen quickly mastered cornhole while Clara and Hadley clapped. She suspected he'd played sports in school. After a couple more games of cornhole, they moved on to the darts. "Ah, a game of precision," Jurgen said, showing his little girl how to hold the darts. "Now Clara you must hit the circle within the circle."

Hadley and Jurgen exchanged a glance. Thank goodness the targets were arranged on a long backdrop of straw.

As he taught little Clara, Jurgen sent his darts sailing. "I think you're familiar with this game," Hadley laughed as they neatly hit their mark.

"Yes. In my free time."

"What is it you do again?" Maybe she'd missed it.

"What I do…" He hit another bull's-eye and turned. In the sunlight his eyes were not brown, as she'd thought earlier, but had interesting flecks of green and gold.

What had they been saying? She blinked. Oh, right. His line of work. "Your livelihood. Do you have a different word for it in

German?" She picked up her own set of darts.

Narrowing his eyes, Jurgen threw another bull's eye. "We live near Bavaria. Starengard."

"Right." She would have to do some googling. Where exactly was Bavaria? "My geography is rusty."

His eyes swung to hers. "I can teach you."

"What, geography?"

"Yes, for a start." His eyes sparkled. Her cheeks burned, although she refused to read anything into this conversation.

Jurgen waved to Emerson. Now what? That poor man hardly had any time to himself. Getting up from his chair, Emerson walked over. Jorgen handed him his phone. "Would you take some shots of us, please?"

"Of course." Emerson stepped away and focused. Picking up the darts, Jurgen handed one to Hadley. Throwing with such competition made her feel self-conscious but Clara loved to be photographed. Jurgen patiently showed her how to hold the dart and how far to pull her arm back. The little girl twirled around with excitement every time she hit any point on the target.

"Could you send me those pictures, please?" she asked Jurgen after the phone had been returned and Emerson had left. "Memories of our trip." They would be great to post on Facebook.

"But of course. Hand me your phone."

While she watched, Jurgen took her phone and tapped in his own number. Then he selected the shots Emerson had taken and sent them to Hadley. "There you go." With a smile he handed back her phone. She couldn't help but feel that they were forging a friendship.

Clearly enjoying himself, Jurgen returned to playing cornhole with Clara and Emerson retreated to his chair. While they were busy, Hadley rejoined her aunt, stopping on the way back to scoop up two mugs of peppermint hot chocolate from the refreshment bar. She found her aunt sitting next to Emerson, deep in conversation. On his other side, Miss Schmidt had fallen asleep sitting in the sun.

"Oh, how thoughtful," Aunt Ethel said after her first sip of hot chocolate. Hadley handed the other mug to Emerson.

"I really couldn't." He held up a hand.

"Of course you can. It's cold up here." So he took the hot chocolate and she went back to pick up another mug.

"Isn't this just wonderful, Hadley," her aunt said when she returned. The chocolate was deep and rich with just the right amount of peppermint.

"It is. Perfect." Watching Jurgen and Clara together was a treat.

Her aunt's reading material had been tucked under the folds of a European travel magazine. As they sat and sipped, Clara and Jurgen waved to them. Was Jurgen favoring that right foot? In any case, Clara was not giving up. She was not about to let her papa leave the cornhole game.

As she sat there with Emerson and her aunt, Hadley wondered at how comfortable those two seemed with each other. But her aunt, she was learning, knew how to fit in with any group.

Her eyes went back to Jurgen and Clara. Jurgen had such a presence, holding himself with authority. Yes, he was probably the president of some bank and maybe Emerson was his assistant. Kind of like Miranda. The customs were so different over here.

The movement of the ship lulled her into a nap, while beside her Aunt Ethel read or chatted quietly with Emerson.

When it came time to order lunch, Jurgen seemed happy to collapse in the chairs next to them, with Clara at his side. They all placed orders with a staff member and trays quickly arrived. Aunt Ethel and Hadley had ordered sandwiches of cheeses and sausage on rye. To Hadley's surprise and delight, a peanut butter and jelly sandwich was produced for Clara. "I want a pop," Clara said to her father.

"No sugar, Clara. You get too silly," Jurgen said quietly, obviously at a loss. Clara did not like to hear no. The little girl looked crushed and Hadley wanted her to keep eating.

"How about some chocolate milk?" Hadley piped up. "I'm going to order some."

"Wonderful idea." Jurgen waved to the waitress and placed the order. Looking uncertain, Clara didn't protest. If she even tried the chocolate milk, Hadley would be happy.

While they sat there chatting. Hadley felt Clara climb up behind her. She was fooling with the french braids Hadley had taken time with that morning. Now she was glad because the braids kept her long hair in place.

"You have such pretty hair, Hadley."

The longing in the little girl's voice made Hadley wheel around and catch Clara in her arms. "Well, so do you, little lady. Want me to braid your hair?"

"Yes, yes!" she screamed, so loud that a few people turned around and smiled.

"Sit here." She nudged Clara between her knees. Taking a comb from her bag, Hadley began to braid Clara's fine hair. Christmas carols played over the sound system. Was this perfect or what? Her spirits lifted as Clara became more excited.

Aunt Ethel dug into her large tote and produced a mirror, handing it to Clara. Holding it in front of her, Clara watched Hadley's movements intently. With one hand over his eyes to block the sun, Jurgen seemed interested in the process. Emerson produced a pair of aviator sunglasses from somewhere and handed them to Jurgen, who slipped them into place. Okay, that definitely added another dimension to Jurgen's image as a father. *The hot father.*

"Ouch!" Clara cried out, bringing a hand to her head.

"Sorry, sorry." She'd just about yanked that braid from Clara's skull. Looking up she found Jurgen smiling at her. *Time to get back to work.* But she wished she didn't have an audience.

"There now," Hadley said when they were finished. She was pleased with her work. Two tidy french braids patterned Clara's head. Turning her head so she could see herself, Clara almost dropped the mirror. Aunt Ethel salvaged the mirror and tucked it back into her bag.

Clara jumped up and spun around. "Look, Papa. Look how beautiful Hadley has made me."

Folding Clara into his arms, Jurgen kissed her cheek. "Yes, you are beautiful, *leibchen.* Now thank Hadley."

Blushing, Hadley shook her head and tucked the comb back into her bag. "It's nothing, really."

His eyes never left her. "It is everything," Jurgen said quietly. His words warmed her like hot chocolate and left her hands trembling. Hadley knit her fingers tightly together in her lap.

Was Aunt Ethel dabbing her eyes? This was crazy. It was only a hairdo.

Frederick and Eva had wandered over and ordered lunch in the same area. Once in a while they would chat with each other, with Frederick sometimes speaking to Jurgen in German or Bavarian, whichever it was. She noticed that Jurgen always replied in English.

At that point, they were cruising past a castle. Set high on the hill and outlined by the sun, the structure looked magnificent in its antiquity. She could only guess at its history. "Will you just look at that, Clara?" And she pointed. "Isn't that amazing?"

"The castle?"

"Yes. Have you ever read the stories of Cinderella and the Prince who live in the castle or the story Snow White? That fairy tale had a prince too."

"Yes," Clara said with her usual certainty. "The prince and the princess always live in a castle."

"But the castles are going away." Frederick broke into the conversation. "Many of the aristocracy now live in private dwellings. Their historical roles have become outdated."

"What makes you think so?" Jurgen asked casually. "Don't you think royalty bring some value to their country? Some modicum of order and stability?"

"Not really." Frederick shook his head. "The world is changing so quickly. In fifty years all of these castles will have become tourist attractions and nothing more."

To Hadley's surprise, her aunt spoke up. "Although I don't know the particulars of the situation," she began, "I think, as an outsider, that the aristocracy do have a role in society for the reasons Jurgen has mentioned. They offer a sense of history and stability to their people. A reason to be proud. Especially if their leaders are people of integrity."

But Frederick did not look convinced. For a younger man, he certainly had stuffy ideas. But then, what did Hadley know about any of this? She enjoyed reading about the royals. Shortly after that Frederick helped Eva from her chair and they wandered away.

"Anyone for more hot chocolate?" Aunt Ethel asked, pushing herself up. "Think I need a stretch of the legs."

"No thank you," Hadley told her. Aunt Ethel set off, nodding to people as she strolled.

"Your aunt is a very bright woman, isn't she?" Jurgen watched her leave. "Very interested in world affairs."

"Yes, Aunt Ethel stays current on everything. She reads several newspapers every day. I think the library here has them. My Uncle Oscar was like that too."

"Has her husband been gone long?" he asked in an undertone. They were sitting together almost shoulder to shoulder while Clara flipped through a book.

"About eight years now. They were so happy together. Traveled a lot and almost finished each other's sentences. She misses him very much."

"How wonderful. And sad. That kind of relationship is difficult when it ends. Very hard to forget. To move past."

Was he talking about his own or Aunt Ethel's situation? That's when she noticed the two men standing against the railing in plaid shirts and jackets. They might be dressed casually today but she recognized them.

"What is it?" Jurgen followed the direction of her eyes. "Is something wrong?"

"Those men," she whispered. "I think they're secret police or something. I saw them yesterday in the markets. What are they doing on the ship? Are they following us?"

"Really? I doubt it." Turning, Jurgen stared in their direction.

"Yes. See how they talk into their lapels. One of them is doing it right now."

With that, Jurgen beckoned to Emerson. "Would you have a few words with those gentlemen? Just to clarify what their position is here. Hadley thinks they might be secret service. Ridiculous, of course."

"Oh no, you don't have to do that." Hadley didn't want to create an errand for Emerson.

But he was already on his way over and the two men stopped their conversation as he approached. The conversation was quick. Soon Emerson returned and whispered something in Jurgen's ear.

"Yes, they are just with the cruise ship," he told her and Hadley felt herself relax. Maybe she was becoming paranoid. "No need to worry."

They stayed in the sun that day while the ship drifted down the Danube. Christmas carols played over the sound system in several different languages. Hadley gave in to the gentle rhythm of the ship's movement. Why worry about anything?

"Think I need a short nap before dinner," Aunt Ethel said when they returned to their suite later that afternoon.

"Good idea. I'm going to catch up on my emails." Would she have anything more from Brock?

After hanging up her coat, Aunt Ethel turned. "You'll make a wonderful mother, Hadley."

What could she say? "Not everyone thinks so."

"But I can't imagine." Her aunt frowned. "You're such a natural with Clara."

"Maybe. Brock doesn't want children." She drifted to the window so her aunt would not see how upset she was. "That was the breaking point with him or so he said."

"Nonsense. Let's sit." Her nap apparently forgotten, Aunt Ethel took a seat on the sofa and patted the cushion next to her.

Hadley didn't feel like hearing a lecture. But she left the window and sat down.

"You know, Uncle Oscar and I could not have children."

"Really? I never knew." The topic had never been discussed at home. If her mother knew, she'd never said anything. Hadley had always assumed their childlessness had been a choice.

"And I can tell you," she said, "it was the great sadness of our lives together. If we had children, I would not have to borrow the happiness of other couples. He understood that very well as we aged and filled our lives with travel and other activities."

"Yes, you did travel a lot." But Hadley had never thought their exciting jaunts abroad had been an attempt to fill some kind of void.

"When you have your own children, you have a place in life."

"But you always have a place with our family. And you know that. We adore you."

Aunt Ethel fluttered a dismissive hand. "Yes. But in time you will see. Nothing is quite the same as having your own place, your own family making plans for you."

Leaning over, she kissed Aunt Ethel's cheek. "I love you, Auntie. Trust me, we are your family. Leanne, Kevin and me. And everybody else."

"That's very sweet. You're very thoughtful, Hadley, and I appreciate that. But please do not limit your future. Think about this and consider carefully." Then she pushed herself up. "Enough from your old aunt. Time for a nap." Aunt Ethel disappeared into her room and closed the doors.

With that, Hadley posted some of the pictures Jurgen had sent. She smiled to see Clara looking so happy as she tossed the darts. And Jurgen was content to watch his daughter have fun. But when she expanded the shot, Hadley saw that what he was really watching was *her.*

Chapter 13

“Maybe we should get to know other people. You know, sit with new people,” Hadley said to Aunt Ethel as they took the elevator to the main dining room that evening. “After all, the ship has three dining rooms.”

“You are so right. Let’s be adventurous and look for some new people to join tonight.” Her aunt swirled a fringed black shawl over her red dress. She always liked to make an impressive entrance and, in most cases, she succeeded. “Does this have to do with Clara and Jurgen?”

“Not really.” Hadley looked away and studied the elevator buttons. “It has to do with that horrible Frederick and his outdated opinions”

“I agree. Such piffle.”

“Piffle?” Turning, Hadley fought a giggle.

“Yes, an old British phrase.” Her aunt’s lips trembled. “Piffle is like trifle that’s been aged too long. Very unpleasant.”

“You’re making that up.”

“Maybe.” The elevator stopped. Arm in arm, they spilled out, laughing.

But Frederick’s views on society weren’t the problem in

Hadley's eyes. She didn't know if she could stand much more of the couple fawning over each other. The covert loving looks and the private conversations. Call it jealousy or whatever, she was over it.

When they entered the dining room, she cast her eyes around and led Aunt Ethel to a table where an older couple was already seated. "May we join you?"

"Delighted," the man said. Dinner began. When her aunt ordered escargot as a starter, Hadley had a salad. The couple was from Brazil so the conversation was interesting. Although she noticed Jurgen and Clara enter, they came in with Emerson and Miss Schmidt and took a table for four at the window. Jurgen was still limping slightly. Smiling over at Hadley, Clara touched her braids as she took her seat. Although Hadley didn't want to be staring, she was. Glancing over, Jurgen gave her a curt nod and Hadley dropped her eyes.

"Look, there's Clara," she told her aunt.

Her aunt turned around. "Oh, isn't that nice. Clara is finally coming to the dining room."

But Jurgen's limping bothered Hadley. Maybe he would be better off taking dinner in his state room, along with a couple of ibuprofen.

Then the conversation at their table turned back to Brazil. How wonderful to hear about other countries. Certainly that was one of the huge benefits of a cruise like this. But this couple, Juana and Miguel, lived a rather enclosed life. Their condo was behind two walls for security reasons. "We travel quite a lot on these ships,"

Juana said. "Meet a lot of nice people.'

"Cheers us up over the holidays," her husband added.

The couple was so outgoing that conversation flowed easily. The appetizers arrived and wine was poured. Although she noticed Eva and Frederick arriving, they were shown to an intimate table for two. Perhaps they also were tired of the larger group. How did they ever eat when he held her hand constantly? But of course, Eva was such a slim thing. She probably didn't eat much. Sucking in her stomach, Hadley remembered Eva when the main entre arrived. Calling on a great deal of fortitude, she ate only half her salmon.

"Aren't you going to finish that?" Aunt Ethel eyed Hadley's plate.

"I ate too much up on the deck today." Well, that was partially true. She had gone beyond her diet. That fresh air gave her an appetite. And so did the cornhole and the darts. She smiled, remembering. She wondered how many calories a person could work off playing darts. Of course, the action mostly worked her arms. Reaching one hand to her bicep, she checked. Was her muscle firmer? Hard to tell.

"What are you doing, dear?" her aunt whispered.

"Just checking something."

"Not one more question from me."

Although she tried not to stare, Hadley's eyes kept going to Jurgen and Clara. She was amazed when their waiter served Clara what looked like a peanut butter and jelly sandwich. But the plate was sent right back. What was going on? Jurgen did not look pleased and Clara was on the edge of tears.

"Really, Hadley." Her aunt leaned closer. "If you're going to openly stare, we might as well have joined them."

The Brazilian couple left for one of the lounges. "In the evening they have karaoke," Juana told her. "It's a lot of fun."

Miguel shook his head and waved good-bye. "My wife has no mercy. I keep telling her I cannot sing."

"No dessert for me tonight," her aunt told the waitress as they enjoyed decaf. Hadley was relieved. Her determination was flagging. Sometimes it took all her stamina to stay with her diet while her aunt enjoyed the latest Viennese torte or a hazelnut meringue heaped with peaches and chocolate sauce.

When they'd finished their coffee and pushed back their chairs, her aunt casually suggested saying good evening to Jurgen and Clara. "We had such a nice day with them."

So they threaded their way through the tables to where Jurgen and Clara sat. From the politely bored expressions on their faces, Emerson and Miss Schmidt looked as if they had been ready to leave long ago. But Clara was jubilant. "Look at my plate, Hadley. I ate it all." And she pointed.

"She would not let them clear her empty plate," Jurgen said with a tolerant smile. A prouder papa could not be seen anywhere.

"Wonderful," Aunt Ethel said. "And what did you order for dinner tonight?"

Was Jurgen squirming in his chair? Aunt Ethel had not been facing this drama, and Hadley wished she had clued her aunt in about what was going on behind her.

"Peanut butter and jelly," Clara responded, as if say *how could you not know what I eat for dinner?* "But they brought it with the crusts. Papa had to send it back."

"A good girl eats everything on her plate." Miss Schmidt could no longer contain herself. Why was this humorless woman entrusted with Clara's care?

At this point Jurgen pinched the bridge of his nose as if he didn't know where to go next.

"How is your ankle?" Hadley asked him. "Have you recovered from your… sports injury?"

Her comment brought a wry smile from Jurgen. "Almost."

Leaning forward, Clara said in a stage whisper, "Papa tries not to limp. He does not like to limp."

"Really?" A giggle was working its way up Hadley's throat. "Maybe Papa should have a cane."

But Jurgen was not a giggling guy. She could see that. And he'd probably rather die than use a cane. Time to move on. "Well, time to retire." *Retire?* What was she saying? Being on the ship in the old world was beginning to get to her. Even her aunt had turned to pin her with a curious look.

"Why does he employ Emerson and Miss Schmidt?" Hadley grumbled to her aunt as the elevator took them up to the third floor. "What an odd combination."

"Oh, I suppose they have their role in Jurgen's life." Her aunt was a sphinx, staring calmly at the colored buttons that lit up as the elevator rose to the third floor.

What the heck did that mean? "Do you think they're related? Like maybe they're his aunt and uncle?"

"Oh, I think not. Definitely not." The doors opened and the conversation was forgotten.

That night Hadley turned in early but the ping of her email took her from her book. Throwing back the covers, she ran to the desk and her laptop. Yes, a message from Brock. "Glad to see that you're having such a good time. I've been thinking about you. Brock."

And how long had it taken him to respond? Maybe this was the result of the pictures she'd posted that afternoon. Her eyes scanned the words five times before she turned off the light. Each time she looked at the words, she read more into them. Maybe he really missed her. Maybe he was thinking about how unreasonable he'd been. Was he jealous that she was on a cruise ship with her aunt?

Sometimes it was so hard to fall asleep.

***

Over the next three or four days leading up to Christmas, the ship meandered down the Danube, stopping for excursions into colorful towns with friendly people and bustling Christmas markets. The stalls gave her interesting posts for Facebook and brought a great response. First they stopped at Nuremberg, which had a charming market, the largest in Europe, or so the guide said.

Of course they shopped. She bought some ornaments for her mother, sister and sister-in-law. But what would the ornaments remind them of? Maybe she should buy some for herself, although she never took the time to put up a tree. But that could all be different next year. Maybe she'd host Christmas Day dinner in her own home. Hadley had to hold on to that hope.

Yes, if she were here with Brock, maybe they would be choosing ornaments for their own tree. She would put them away for next year, the way her mother did.

As she studied the ornaments, her aunt's words came back to her about borrowing other people's families and their joy. Feeling uncertain now, at the next stall she chose a delicately carved ornament picturing the nativity scene. If she didn't have her own tree next year, she would simply give the ornament away.

In Bamberg, the tour group visited a castle. The walls were thick and the atmosphere, grim. She shivered inside her quilted jacket and wished she had a hat. Apparently this castle had been destroyed in the 16th century. Some of the structure was retained when they rebuilt. She didn't know how she felt about having lunch in a restaurant that was part of the new building but Aunt Ethel got a kick out of it. "We are eating inside history," she said dramatically. And then she asked Hadley to take some pictures.

But as she studied the stonework, Frederick's words came back to Hadley. Were these castles a part of the past? Did they have any place in the future? "The castles were designed to protect the townspeople," the tour guide told them. "The people could see the enemy approaching. And in those days, the armies arrived by boat and set up their armory." Now, that was a chilling statement.

Brock had started emailing her more often—a teasing back-and -forth rally that reminded her of when they'd first met. She started to miss him. The more she posted on Facebook, the more he emailed her.

"Are you going to buy me anything at one of the markets?" he asked in an email after one of her excursions.

Was she? She thumbed the ring still on her finger. What would be right for him? If it was too expensive, he might accuse her of wasting money. If it was something like a mug, he might tease her about bringing back a knickknack. That was what he called the memorabilia in her parents' home. Did she even know her fiancé? And more importantly, did she like him?

In the mornings, she ran around the outdoor track or visited the fitness center. But she felt curiously disappointed when she didn't run into Jurgen at either spot. His ankle must still be bothering him and she hoped he'd gone to the ship's physician.

"Will you be going on the trip to Prague?" she asked when she saw Jurgen and Clara in the dining room one evening. The crumbs on Clara's plate indicated that she had once again finished a peanut butter and jelly sandwich.

"Yes, we are planning on it," Jurgen said. "But we may have to rest sometimes."

Clara patted her father's hand. "Papa is my patient."

"Miss Schmidt will be coming of course," Jurgen said, his eyes sliding to Clara.

"The rule maker with the rule breaker," Hadley muttered to her aunt as they said good night and went back to their suite.

"Why, you'd fit right in, dear," Aunt Ethel said.

Now, what did that mean?

Chapter 14

Hadley and her aunt were excited about the side trip to Prague. "Wait until you see their old town," her aunt said at dinner one night. They happened to be sitting with Jurgen and Clara. Although sometimes Miss Schmidt and Emerson came along, this time when Clara had come dashing toward them through the dining room without the other two, Hadley felt pleased. No way could she say that they wanted to be alone. And Aunt Ethel seemed to feel the same. She obviously liked being with Clara and Jurgen. The little girl made her smile.

"Is the town pretty?" Clara asked, her eyes glowing.

"Yes, very beautiful." Her aunt had that distant look in her eye. "And it has been for a very long time." Hadley exchanged a look with Jurgen. She knew that her aunt was thinking of visiting with Uncle Oscar. By this time Jurgen was aware of that too.

"Will they have more elves here?"

"Maybe," Aunt Ethel said mysteriously.

"I want to go too, Papa." Always so dramatic, Clara tented her hands into a praying position. "Can we go too?"

"We have tickets for that trip. But the bus trip to reach the city takes more time than the other excursions–one or two hours. Can you sit still for all that time?" Jurgen looked doubtful.

"Maybe we can sing Christmas carols," Clara said, gazing up at Hadley. "The way we did that one time. Hadley, can we sing with you, please?"

Hadley had to chuckle. She didn't have a great voice. "If you can stand to listen, then yes, we can sing."

"We enjoy listening to your singing," Jurgen said.

Ah huh. He was probably just being polite. His manners were impeccable. Very old school and she was discovering that she liked that. Very much.

The next day they got up for an early start on that long bus ride. "Wear your warm clothes," her aunt said, pulling on her winter coat with the fur collar. "The winds can be quite cold when we're walking around." She swathed her head in a pretty paisley scarf.

But Hadley didn't want to bundle up in a long coat for that ride. It would be too warm on the bus. So she pulled on her quilted jacket with black stretch pants and boots. Underneath, she wore a red sweater. "And don't forget your passport, Hadley," her aunt said. "We'll be in another country."

Going back into her private apartment, Hadley punched in the code to her safe and retrieved her passport. She was glad Aunt Ethel had reminded her. Where was her mind these days? Every time her email pinged, Hadley had to run and read it. Miranda sent her an update every couple of days but it was Brock's emails that she pored over.

But her fiancé never had much to say. Not really. How she longed to read that he missed her. Or that he had reconsidered and wanted to apologize about their disagreement that day over lunch. But those words never came.

When they reached the reception area downstairs, people were gathered in excited clusters. Outside, Clara and Jurgen stood waiting for them. Clara waved to her to hurry up. Quickly, the four of them climbed onto the second bus. "Thank goodness for these comfortable seats," Aunt Ethel said, settling back.

Jurgen and Clara took the seats behind them. After a little while, all three buses were full and they pulled away. Christmas carols provided a cheerful backdrop as the bus gained speed and gradually turned onto one of the highways. If the language was familiar, many of the people sang along. Everyone recognized and sang "Oh Tannenbaum" in their own language.

Halfway through the trip, their guide came down the aisle with a basket of prettily wrapped packages of Christmas cookies and small foil boxes of chocolates. Although she didn't realize that Jurgen was a sweet freak, he took both and then carefully slid them into the pocket of his seat. Excited by any new experience, Clara asked for both also.

Hope rose in Hadley's heart. Could Clara be tempted by these beautifully decorated cookies? Granted they had little food value but they could signal a beginning. But no, following her father's lead, the little girl stowed them in the seat pocket. Ripping open her cookies, Hadley began to nibble.

"Isn't this wonderful?" Aunt Ethel giggled, opening her cookie packet too. She definitely loved her snacks. "Why take a cruise like this if you were not going to participate in all the amenities?"

"Why indeed," came Jurgen's voice from behind them. "We must taste test everything."

Her aunt and Jurgen were quite the pair. As Christmas carols played overhead, the bus traveled down the highways. Light snow started to fall and the windshield wipers quickly dispatched the feathery stuff. Hadley couldn't remember when she'd felt more Christmasy.

When the bus pulled up at the appointed drop-off point, Aunt Ethel encouraged them to bypass the nearest Christmas market. "I would suggest that we go to one of the main shopping streets on Charles Bridge." Hadley had to smile at how they'd become a group of four.

"Excellent idea," Jurgen said. "Clara, take my hand. There are too many people here and they crowd too close."

"If I remember correctly, I think I know one thing that will please you very much," Aunt Ethel told Clara. "And I would like to buy it for you for Christmas."

"A Christmas present for me?" Clara's face lit up.

"There is no need for that." Jurgen seemed to take offense.

"Just a little gift." Bustling along, Aunt Ethel took no notice of Jurgen's comment. "Christmas has nothing to do with needs. If that were the case, we would all be eating baked potatoes on Christmas day, but we're not. No, Christmas is about the finer things. The things that speak to your heart."

What was her aunt talking about? As usual, Clara soon broke free from her father. The little girl started making the rounds, jumping from one stall to another. Jurgen had his hands full trying to keep track of his daughter. Aunt Ethel kept teasing her about the mystery gift if she were good. But that veiled threat didn't slow Clara down.

As they approached the stores on Charles Bridge, Hadley spotted the marionettes. Why of course, her aunt would think of these. You couldn't miss the colorful puppets. Right now they were surrounded by children. From the way Aunt Ethel was smiling, this was the gift she'd been talking about. When her turn came, Clara took her time choosing. While Jurgen, Aunt Ethel and Clara were busy comparing the marionettes, Hadley wandered over to look at the colorfully decorated shop windows and did some of her own Christmas shopping.

One of the store windows displayed exquisite Bohemian cut glass. Going inside, she chose a piece she knew her mother would love to have in the living room. Her brother and sister would have to warn their children about it. While Aunt Ethel and Jurgen were having their purchases wrapped up, Hadley had the bowl sent to her parents.

After that, they walked from the bridge while her aunt studied the street signs. When they had reached a certain point, Aunt Ethel turned to Jurgen. "I wonder if you could take Clara down the street for a cup of hot chocolate. I have an errand to run with Hadley. We'll meet you back at the marionette stand."

"Are you going to buy Hadley a present?" Clara asked as her dad tried to pull her away.

"Clara, really," Jurgen said, although he seemed curious too.

Her aunt nodded. "You are so right, Clara. For New Year's

Eve."

"Oh, no, Aunt Ethel. Not for New Year's Eve." That was ridiculous. "We don't even know what we'll be doing."

"But of course." To her frustration, Jurgen jumped right on the bandwagon as the shoppers brushed past them on the busy street. "New Year's Eve on board ship is a very grand affair. You'll enjoy it, Hadley."

"Can I be there?" Clara asked.

"Maybe." Bending over, Jurgen looked deep into his daughter's eyes. "If you are a very good girl."

The warning brought a sigh from Clara and an impatient stamp of her black boots. "First I have to be good for Santa and then I have to be good for New Year's Eve. That's not fair."

Jurgen roared while Aunt Ethel and Hadley joined in.

Her aunt was already leading her away and Hadley had to follow. With a wave goodbye, they left Jurgen and Clara to go their own way. New Year's Eve held no magic for her. Without Brock, the coming year wouldn't be at all what she'd planned.

But she couldn't disappoint her aunt. The more time she spent with her, the more she realized that Aunt Ethel got her fun out of doing things for other people.

"What did you have in mind?" A cold wind blew through the narrow cobblestone streets. She envied Aunt Ethel's warm scarf around her head. Hadley's ears were stinging. As they walked, they didn't stop to window shop. Aunt Ethel knew exactly where she was headed and kept her eyes fixed straight ahead.

"Yes. Here we are." Finally, Aunt Ethel paused to study a

window.

Elka's Gowns was scripted in gold on the windows of this charming little shop. The long dresses in the window took Hadley's breath away. “Oh no. I couldn't.” But she drew closer.

Her aunt already had one hand on the door. “I brought a gown for New Year's Eve with me and you simply must have one too. We’ll celebrate with the wonderful people we met over these two weeks. That's customary at the end of a cruise, especially on New Year’s Eve.”

Well, there was no way around this. A bell above the door jingled when Aunt Ethel pushed it open. The rush of warm air drew Hadley inside. She would be foolish to protest. And on top of that, a little crazy. The shop itself promised to be a memorable experience.

Elka’s Shop smelled of oranges, cinnamon and all wonderful things. Feathered fans, long gloves and costume jewelry were displayed under glass. Dresses protected in plastic hung temptingly on racks. Hadley couldn’t resist. She edged closer. This was a carefully curated collection, or so a tastefully small sign indicated. She could only imagine what these dresses cost. The tags only indicated size. A woman of about fifty came bustling from the back. “May I help you?” she said in charmingly accented English.

“Yes, we've come for a special gown.” With this, Aunt Ethel turned toward her. “For my niece.”

Surely this was a dream. Hadley was not really standing in a shop in front of the most beautiful dresses she’d ever seen. Well, besides her wedding gown, which she might never wear.

"Certainly." Wearing a delighted smile, the woman turned toward her. "I am Elka, my dear. And I will help you choose a gown that is more wonderful than anything you have ever worn in your life."

Now, that was quite a promise. But this woman certainly seemed up to the challenge. By then Elka was circling her. Sucking in her stomach, Hadley held her breath. Her aunt had settled into a high-backed chair tufted in lilac velvet, and a woman named Mariana appeared with a pot of tea and biscuits.

Elka led her to one of the large fitting rooms. That's when Hadley knew the front of the shop was just for show. The magic happened back in this room. Somehow her jacket was slipped from her shoulders and whisked away, along with her sweater and slacks. A tape measure materialized. Elka now wore a look of concentration as she took measurements while Mariana noted the numbers on a pad. Never once did the dear woman scold her for having a bit of fat here or a curve there. "Perfect," Elka said when she was satisfied.

"I've been trying to lose weight."

Elka studied her hips. "Ridiculous. You could use a few more pastries. This gown is for New Year's," Elka said to Mariana. "We will need the…" Here she rattled off a range of European sizes. The colors she threw out got Hadley dreaming. Sea green, celestial white, silvery gray and winsome blue.

"We're from one of the cruise ships." Aunt Ethel had wandered back, a teacup in one hand.

"But we're dieting," Hadley interjected. "Well, I am. Trying."

Both women shrieked with laughter, as if that was the funniest thing they'd ever heard. As if Hadley had unwittingly revealed how young she was, how inexperienced and how very foolish.

"On a cruise ship," Elka said, wiping the tears from her eyes. "And you're attempting to diet. Oh, you are so funny."

"Exactly," her aunt agreed.

"Now, Mrs. Romerly, this is to be a surprise." Was Elka really banning her aunt from the dressing room? And how did she know her aunt's last name?

"Well then, I'll be waiting out front," her aunt sang out as she wandered back to the front room, snatching a macaroon from a nearby dish.

It didn't take long at all for Mariana to return with gowns that rustled and whispered of magical things about to begin. "Oh, not for me. I couldn't wear these." As she cowered against the three-way mirror, she couldn't help reaching out. Could she just touch one? But not before Mariana had fitted a white cotton glove over each hand. These were gowns that could appear in the movies. Audrey Hepburn came to mind along with Ava Gardner and the many other glamourous movie stars that got Aunt Ethel sighing when she watched the classic movies.

Elka was already unzipping and unbuttoning while Hadley stood there trembling. Then the best Christmas present of all began. In preparation Mariana swept Hadley's blonde hair up into a style that still left hair curling down her back. "So beautiful," Mariana murmured.

How long had it been since anyone complimented her about

her hair? She turned to face the mirror. Facing her was a young woman she didn't recognize. Hadley glanced down at the ring on her finger. Oh yes this was her. She was the jilted bride-to-be that had escaped into this magical world to reassess her life.

And how am I coming with that?

The choosing began. The icy blue dress with a skirt that Cinderella would have worn as she escaped from the ball made Hadley look a bit remote, snooty even. Aunt Ethel shook her head when Hadley modeled the gown for her. "Lovely, but not you." Hadley agreed.

The more fitted sea green gown could have been worn by a mermaid as she swam in the sea. The aqua underlay was made luminous by a glittery, pale green netting that spoke of warm waters and wonderful things. But Hadley didn't quite like the fit of it. When she turned the skirt did not billow around her. "I'm not sure. Aunt Ethel?"

Crunching into another cookie, her aunt shook her head. "Let's keep looking."

So the mermaid dress was hung on a hook. The black gown with all the draping was much too serious. "Like Morticia," Hadley said as she turned for her aunt. "I could be dangerous in this."

The older women laughed together. The aqua was a possibility but it spoke of summer days—not a winter's night when fireworks would explode in the dark sky above, with horns blaring and people cheering. The next year would be better. Wasn't that what New Year's Eve was about? Hope and oh, how she wanted that, along with happiness.

As Elka helped her out of a yellow gown that definitely wasn't her, Marianna swept the curtain aside. "Just in," she said to Elka knowingly, holding out another gown.

"Ah, yes." When the shopkeeper took and twisted the hanger in her hand, the skirt swished and whispered invitingly. The fabric moved with a life that any young woman would want to claim. It suggested possibilities, along with the knowledge that all dreams would be granted. Elka unzipped the back and Hadley stepped into it.

"Wait until you see what's coming," Elka called out to the front of the store.

"I'm going to close my eyes now," Aunt Ethel answered, as if she knew what had arrived. Really, she could be so cute. For a second Hadley felt a little sad that Kevin and Leanne could not see this playful part of Aunt Ethel. She would have to take care of this when they were home.

The dress was zipped. And over the placket was a row of delicate covered buttons. Turning to the mirror, Hadley felt transported. "Why I never… I just couldn't… Is this me?"

Elka led her to the front. With a gasp, Aunt Ethel put down her teacup and began to weep. "Oh yes, my dear," she sniffed, dabbing at her eyes. "This is you. And *this* is the gown."

The underlay was silk of a pale silver hue called moonlight. Delicate flowers patterned the sheer overlay that fell to the floor. No V-neck had ever looked this flattering on Hadley and the sleeves were the same—long but see-through with flowers tracing down each arm. A scattering of pearls and sequins made the dress gleam and sparkle when she turned. So she twirled, she sat, and then she stood to twirl again. Yes, the gown had been made for her.

Feeling as if she were living a dream, Hadley changed back into her street clothes. When she reached the outer showroom, Aunt Ethel wore a satisfied smile. Elka was telling her that "the dress will be in Vienna in two days, with the alterations made. The Hotel Sacher." Her aunt rattled off the name of someone at that hotel, as if she were sending the dress to her own address at home.

Hadley almost hated to leave the shop, but Jurgen and Clara were waiting. As she was hustled back outside, flakes of snow melted on her cheeks because it had been so warm and cozy inside Elka's shop.

When they reached the stall for the marionettes, the crowd had thinned. Jurgen and Clara were apparently being given a lesson by the man who sold the puppets. But Hadley laughed to see Clara's fingers wound up in the cords. "Where were you?" she asked. "You missed all the fun."

"Trust me, I had a lot of fun too." Hadley smiled at her aunt.

As the shop keeper repacked the two marionettes they'd bought earlier, Jurgen turned to her with a curious look. "Are you all right? You look pale."

"It's just the cold." She held her stinging ears between her mittened hands.

"I know just the thing." Grabbing the bag from the gentleman, Jurgen took Clara's hand. "Clara chose this for you while you were gone. Our Christmas present."

"Oh, my goodness." There were way too many gifts coming her way. They came to a corner display of hats and scarves.

"Look!" Clara pointed to a red cap topped with a silver gray pom-pom. "This will match your sweater and boots."

Jurgen motioned to the woman who was standing there smiling, although her nose was red from the cold.

"I really couldn't. You're all impossible." But of course Jurgen and Clara wouldn't listen to her and her aunt didn't come to her aid either. When she slipped the cap onto her head, Hadley's ears stopped throbbing. "This hat is wonderfully warm. But you'll have to speak up. The knit is so thick."

"And now I think lunch is in order." Jurgen said as he handed a card to the woman.

"The hat becomes you," Aunt Ethel said. But the woman had returned with Jurgen's card.

"Didn't I give you the right one?" Jurgen looked puzzled. "I am not very good with this."

Oh dear. Embarrassed, Hadley tugged her aunt away so they wouldn't be overheard. "Maybe he's charged up to his limit?" She certainly didn't want to be responsible for that. And yet weren't Jurgen and Clara in the suite up on the third floor?

Aunt Ethel linked her arm through Hadley's. "I don't think that's the situation at all. So now, what about lunch?"

Chapter 15

"This way, ladies. I think we all need food." Jurgen had had enough shopping for today. His ankle was starting to act up and Clara was getting testy—usually a sign that she was hungry. He knew just the place. Shepherding the ladies in front of him, they made their way through the crowded streets. On the day before Christmas, everyone was doing last minute shopping. He was so pleased that he had that covered. Sometimes he really missed having Emerson with him. He might have to rethink giving his valet the day off for these excursions. Emerson was always ready to offer the royal credit cards, when needed.

After they'd been seated at one of his favorite cafes, he spoke quietly to a waiter about Clara's needs. Hadley and her aunt studied the menu intently. They took their food so seriously that he almost laughed. Clara had been right. That brilliant red hat with the oversized silver pom-pom was perfect for Hadley. She looked like a teenager wearing that hat. But on her left hand twinkled an engagement ring. That ridiculous stone and its equally ostentatious setting were beginning to bother him.

She was worthy of more. The thought hit him with such force that the menu slipped from his fingers.

"Papa." Clara nudged him and looked pointedly at the worn wooden floor. "You dropped something."

His little girl seemed so pleased to catch him in one of his awkward moments. "Yes, yes. I am a clumsy oaf. Right, *liebchen*?"

The *schnitzel* and *eintopf* were quickly brought to the table, along with Clara's peanut butter sandwich. Thank heavens the pleasant waitress found some plain white bread that they kept for tourists. The textured German breads were much more popular, but not with Clara. As they ate, the aroma of good, healthy food filled the air. And the potato salad? Never had he tasted anything so fine. The flavorful vinegar and oil combination with bacon bits was, in his eyes, a welcome contrast to the mayonnaise potato salad Americans favored. He did not allow it on his ships.

Luckily, the peanut butter and jelly sandwich seemed to be universal. But Clara was more interested in Hadley and her aunt than her own food. With her eyes on the two women, she ate mindlessly. The knot in his chest—that bothered him only when he ate with his daughter—loosened.

"What did you buy on your secret trip?" Clara asked at one point.

Laughing, Hadley glanced over at her aunt. She was so devoted to the older woman. Her attention was very touching. "I can't tell," she finally said, blushing.

The color in her cheeks made Jurgen curious. "What kind of shop did you visit, if I may ask?"

Wagging a finger, Ethel Romerly began to laugh. "If we tell you that, you might figure it all out. Tick a lock." Here, Ethel made a strange motion on her lips with her fingers.

"What kind of lock?" Clara asked.

"Just an old saying." With a shake of her head, Hadley slid her eyes to her aunt. Did she realize that Clara might think she was laughing at her? Very sensitive woman.

"The secret will be revealed," her aunt told Clara.

"When?" Clara would not let this go. Their plates were empty. He checked his watch. They should move on and he stood.

"Would you like the check?" The waitress was back.

"Check?" Surprised, he turned and nodded. Well, he'd almost walked off without paying. And that would "blow his cover," as those James Bond movies said. But now he had to dig out one of those credit cards Emerson had given him. The ladies dashed inside to the restroom, taking Clara with them. As they disappeared, a woman on the street turned toward him. "Isn't that…" She asked her companion in a loud voice.

Quickly, Jurgen ducked his head and turned away. If he were recognized, there would be problems. His security detail, however, had noticed. He saw Ernst speak into his lapel alerting the other one, Hans. Hadley and her aunt could not know who he was. So far, the trip had been so refreshing without the weight of the crown on his head. And he was having such a good time with Clara away from his mother's scrutiny.

Ah, yes, the ladies were back, the three of them threading their way through the tables while Clara chattered away. The waitress returned. He scrawled his signature on the slip and they were off. Their stomachs full, they wandered back to old town to "check out," as Hadley put it, one of the historical churches. Their footsteps echoed on century-old tiles amid the smell of incense—both part of his upbringing. Of course the church was decorated for the holidays. The main attraction seemed to be a beautiful nativity scene that must have been centuries old. Hadley and her aunt took their time and he was gratified to see the respect they had for the past. Standing there, he said his own prayer.

Then they were back on the street. Clara was drawn to some colorful posters for *The Nutcracker,*" which was playing in Prague. The advertising was beautifully done.

"Look, Hadley. The ballerina looks like you!" His little girl pointed to the poster where the Sugar Plum Fairy was pictured in full flight with her partner. This production had been one of Liesel's favorites around the holidays. Jurgen had seen it with her many times. Clara was just reaching the age when she could appreciate this classic when her mother was taken from them.

"Have you seen *The Nutcracker*?" Hadley asked Clara. She seemed amazed when his little girl shook her head. Reaching up, Clara traced the graceful motion of the ballerina's arm with a finger. Guilt enveloped Jurgen as he stood there on the busy street. Would he spend the rest of his life feeling the weight of what he had failed to do?

"Really? I would think living over here you would have seen it, my dear," Hadley's aunt chimed in, turning to him.

"Sometimes I can't keep up with it all." That was all he could come up with? To discourage further questioning, he studied the poster of the Sugar Plum Fairy.

"Oh, I know, I know." Aunt Ethel patted his arm. "So many responsibilities. In your situation, I mean."

Jurgen resisted the impulse to hug Hadley's unpredictable, outspoken aunt. She understood.

As they moved farther down the street, an idea formed in his head. Sometimes he felt clueless. But he might still have time to plan something wonderful.

This was the best Christmas Eve Day he'd had in a long time. The clock on the church indicated it was still early. They didn't have to be back to the bus until three. As they passed the City Hall, he spotted children and their parents ice-skating on a public rink just across the street. A light snow had begun falling again. The effect was charming. Laughter floated on the air, along with the muted sound of the skate blades whisking across the ice.

Hadley drew closer to the fencing. "Oh look. Ice skating. That looks like fun, doesn't it?"

"I think you would end up on your behind in no time at all." The words were out before he could consider them. In the past such mistakes had not bothered him. But with Hadley, they did. A gentleman does not refer to a woman's "behind."

"How is your ankle?" Hadley asked innocently. But her reddened cheeks told another story. Had she noticed that he didn't join her on the track in the morning? Or show up in the fitness center? He wished she would miss him. The thought unnerved him.

What was it about this woman who wore her engagement ring with such sad indifference? She was funny and so kind, not just to

Clara, but to her aunt. He wanted to get to know her better.

Jurgen was not about to admit that nurturing his ankle had become a ruse. With a little rest, it would be perfectly fine. Emerson had brought Jurgen's private surgeon on the trip and he had assessed the ankle with maddening care. Jurgen was having trouble with the "rest" part. And so, he had been avoiding the track and the fitness center.

As dawn broke beyond the heavy drapes, he would roll over in his bed and go back to sleep. Without the duties of the kingdom calling for his attention, extending his rest felt like such a luxury. Jurgen was actually enjoying it.

That is, unless he began to think about Hadley. Her beautiful hair twisted into elegant braids. The crazy laugh she didn't try to hide. Her unabashed candor. And Clara's excitement every time Hadley came on the scene. Yes, that had affected him deeply.

Now Hadley fluttered her lashes up at him while the snow patterned the hat they'd given her. Was she flirting with him? The cold restored his senses. Of course she wasn't. She was engaged and he gave his head a quick shake. "Pardon me?"

"Your ankle?" She glanced down at his boots. He didn't want to admit that his right ankle was aching from all the walking. Jurgen hardly felt the pain every time he looked at her smile.

"Coming along nicely."

"Papa, Papa. I want to skate!" Clara pulled at his jacket. "Can I, please?"

"But you have no skates and you don't know how. What if you fall?"

"You mean you live in this cold weather and you don't ice skate?" Hadley grinned with delight at catching him in another shortcoming. "Clara can't be hurt if she falls in the snow. Besides, I'll be there to catch her."

Two could play at this game. "And you skate, I suppose?"

"As a matter of fact, yes. In the Midwest the winters are long and cold. During the winter months, we brought our skates to school. When classes ended, we'd grab our skates from the cloakroom and run across the street to the outdoor rink."

How incredibly free. She did not have to worry about security or checking protocol with anyone. It sounded as if Hadley lived a charmed life. Still, there was that sadness in her eyes.

They'd drawn closer to the rink and Hadley pointed to the warming hut. "I'll bet they rent skates there." She grinned at him and he took that as a challenge. Clara would never forgive him if he said no and they had the time.

"I'll hold her," Hadley told him. "Keep her from falling."

"How perfect," Aunt Ethel said, while Hadley waited for his decision. How could he refuse?

"All right. I guess so."

"Such enthusiasm." Hadley giggled, taking Clara's hand. "Come on. We'll show your papa, right?"

Minutes later, Hadley was leading Clara out onto the rink. He was glad to see that she held Clara tightly by the hands. Once they reached the ice, Hadley turned around on her rented skates and pulled Clara gently toward her.

"Hadley can skate backwards!" Clara called out, her voice

carrying on the cold winter air.

"Hadley's a very talented young woman," her Aunt Ethel said, sitting down on one of the benches. The poor woman must be exhausted. "My, do I smell hot chocolate?"

Although he hated to leave this extraordinary sight, Ernest and Hans had arrived. They would keep an eye on Clara. He dashed inside and quickly returned with two cups of hot chocolate. Sitting down on the bench, he left his cup in the snow next to his boots. Inside he'd had to go through the whole ridiculous process of the plastic card. How clever of both Emerson and Miss Schmidt to stay back at the ship today. Independence had its price or so he was learning. They took care of so many details for him.

"Is everything all right?" He handed Ethel her hot chocolate.

"Wonderful." Her eyes glowed as she watched her niece.

Jurgen searched the rink until he found the bright red hat with the silver pom-pom.

Steering Clara toward the edge of the crowd, Hadley skated behind his daughter, holding her securely. Eyes wide, Clara laughed with delight. It was no surprise to him that his child was fearless. Together they circled the outer ring, safely skirting the more adventurous children. Some raced, circled and even did jumps in the center of the large rink.

Perhaps he should have one put in at the palace. Wouldn't it be nice if Clara could skate with other children her age? Certainly there were people on staff who would be glad to have their children use the rink. He would buy them all skates.

Leaning forward on his elbows, Jurgen was mesmerized. Out in the cold with her cheeks cherry red and that ridiculously large pom-pom bobbing from her hat, Hadley could have been Clara's older sister. How old was she anyway? He had married Liesel when she was so young, barely twenty, and he had been in his early thirties. Childbearing was easier at that age or so they'd been told so they started their family without delay, unaware that other dangers could lurk silently.

Throwing back her head, Clara tried to catch the snowflakes on her tongue. Giggling, Hadley did the same. Beside him, Ethel watched intently while she sipped the chocolate.

"They are like children together, aren't they?" he murmured.

"Yes," she said. "Hadley is enjoying herself today." But then a shadow passed over the aunt's face. Whatever was bothering Hadley, her aunt was well aware of it too.

Clara's laughter carried through the cold air, reminding him of his own childhood. He wanted her to enjoy these early years like normal children. Hadn't he promised Liesel? His own upbringing had been so structured. Painfully so. And if he followed his mother's directives, Clara might experience the same in a boarding school. With each passing day, he now realized that he could never let that happen.

When the overhead lights snapped on around the rink, an appreciative murmur passed through the crowd. The dramatic glow also struck the cathedral and the other buildings nearby. Bundled up in her winter coat and scarf, Hadley's aunt nodded off once or twice. They should leave. After throwing away their empty cups, Jurgen motioned to his two skaters.

"Wait," Hadley said after they turned in their skates. The snow was falling faster. Mounds had formed around the skating rink. "We have to make angels."

"Angels?" Clara clapped her mittens together.

And with that, Hadley fell back into a mound of snow. Her arms flailed wildly. He had seen this once in one of those Hallmark Christmas movies Liesel enjoyed. By the time he'd come to his senses, Clara was also on her back in the snow. His security detail came closer, either out of curiosity or concern.

Giving a stern shake of his head, he drew closer and pulled out his phone.

"Do you know how to take a picture with that?" Ethel was there at his elbow.

"Of course." Emerson had given him a lesson recently. He wanted to have a lot of pictures of Clara. He'd been remiss in that. Now he snapped away and even made a video as their arms and legs arced in the snow. His daughter laughed and laughed, happier than he'd ever seen her.

The pictures would give him a lot to think about. "Time to leave." He pocketed his phone. After brushing the snow from Clara so she wouldn't become chilled on the bus, he turned to Hadley. The cold had heightened her color. Her beauty stunned him. "You…you have snow on your hat."

"I do? What a surprise." Eyes sparkling, she laughed up at him.

Aunt Ethel was busy with Clara when Jurgen gently brushed the snow from the red hat. But he wanted to do more. Like gently kiss her lips. Like cup her cold cheeks in his warm hands. Like open his heart to feelings he hadn't allowed himself for so long.

But not now. If ever. Turning away, he took Clara's hand.

On the way back to the ship, Hadley and her aunt found seats towards the back. Jurgen and Clara took a seat on the other side. Cuddling next to him, Clara seemed overstimulated and talkative. "Do you want to know what Hadley told me while we were skating?"

He certainly did. "And what would that be?"

"She wore lipstick for the first time ever at the ice skating rink." Clearly Clara was very excited by that. "And her parents never even punished her."

Jurgen swallowed a laugh. He should take this girl stuff seriously. "Maybe her parents didn't know. Did you share our rules with Hadley?"

Clara's smile dissolved into a very serious expression. "Yes, I told her that you would not let me wear make up until I was sixteen."

"I'm sure she found that very sensible."

"She laughed. Hadley thought that was really funny." Clara yawned and Jurgen pulled her closer. These fancy braids Hadley had created for his daughter were very pretty. But not something he could ever handle. Sometimes he felt he was not up to the task of being the single parent. But he was trying to catch up.

Clara fell asleep, eyelashes feathered across her cheeks. When his little girl slept, she looked like an angel. Over the last few days, she'd been so much happier.

Tomorrow was Christmas. Sitting back, Jurgen somehow knew

it would be a Christmas like one he'd never had before.

Chapter 16

Turning over in her silky smooth, six-hundred-thread sheets, Hadley detected the faint scent of cinnamon and smiled. Yesterday Aunt Ethel had gone crazy in the salon with some pine cones she'd picked up in Prague. Then it hit her. *Christmas.* She slid down under the comforter. The dreaded day was here. And she felt happy. Content. Reaching for the remote on her bedside table, she pressed Open. The drapes parted. Another button and the sheers slid aside. This cruise could really spoil her.

Outside a light snow had dressed the countryside in white. Smoked curled from a house and she pictured a family sitting down for an ample breakfast of sausages, eggs and pastries. She was starving. Another touch of her remote and the sheers came together with a whisper.

Instead of the dread she'd expected, Hadley looked forward to the day with a warm cozy feeling. Yesterday had been so wonderful in Prague. Even if she never got to wear that exquisite dress in the states, she would wear it on New Year's Eve to please Aunt Ethel. And herself. So outrageous, but that gorgeous gown made her feel beautiful.

The feel of silk on her skin, the swish of the long skirt and the elegant look of her arms in those sleeves—she wanted some pictures to show her family. And maybe to post on Facebook. And because the dress had a subtly higher waistline, she could feel free to eat what she liked today. She would not be on a diet. That was her Christmas gift to herself today.

But now she had to get her metabolism going. Patting her pillow good-bye, she pushed back the covers and sprang from the bed. After brushing her teeth, she pulled her hair up into a high ponytail. Then she pulled on her running pants and zipped up a jacket over the T-shirt that said "It's fun to run!" Tucking her keycard into her waistband, she slipped out the door and took the stairs down to the second floor.

Outside on the track the air was bracing. Some would say it was freezing cold. But here, people seem to take on the weather with gusto. After she got going, she'd warm up fast. Beginning with her slow pace, she ran the length of the track, accelerating as she rounded the curves. How wonderful to have the track to herself. Then she saw a figure jogging slowly up ahead. Jurgen? Really? His ankle must be feeling better. She was surprised that he'd made it through all the walking yesterday.

Yesterday. What a wonderful time she'd had with Clara. And if she were honest with herself, she'd enjoyed watching Jurgen with his little girl. He was loving and protective—everything you would want in a father. Yes, sometimes he could be grumpy. Jurgen didn't like to be teased, not that his occasional grumpy mood stopped her. Hadley enjoyed watching the color creep into his cheeks. Could he feel it? Did he hate it? She loved seeing his outrageously long lashes flutter as he considered what to say. And that clenching in his jaw? She found it fascinating.

But enough of this. Hadley picked up the pace.

As she drew closer, Jurgen looked back over his shoulder. The surprise and dismay on his face made her laugh. But he slowed down as they approached a seating cluster, one hand reaching for the back of a chair. He couldn't fool her. That ankle was hurting. "Merry Christmas, Jurgen."

"Merry Christmas." He smiled down on her. "*Frohe Weihnachten.*"

"Okay, same to you, but don't ask me to repeat that." For a second they stood there, grinning at each other. Her imagination ran wild. Every time she saw him like this, she found him more attractive.

"I had a wonderful time yesterday with you and your aunt," he finally said.

Memories from that special day warmed her. "Me too, and I know Aunt Ethel enjoyed herself."

"Clara loves to spend time with you." A breeze whipped off the water, lifting his dark hair, while he tried to flatten it. She was glad Jurgen wore his hair long. She wouldn't look down at his strong legs or the way his muscled chest rose and filled with each breath. It was rude to stare. But maybe just one quick peek and Hadley rubbed the back of her neck so he wouldn't notice the glance.

When she lifted her gaze, she found Jurgen staring at her left hand. Suddenly self-conscious, she rubbed the back of her ring finger with her thumb. "Merry Christmas." That was all she could say today? She stared up at him so handsome even in this freezing weather. His full lips quirked up at the corners.

He chuckled under his breath. "Yes, you said that already. And Merry Christmas to you too. You have made Clara so much happier this Christmas." Here words seem to fail him. Or maybe she just didn't hear them because her heart was beating so loudly. "I cannot thank you enough. That might sound silly. But the past week? You have made a difference in Clara's life."

The words had cost him. She could see that. And she wanted to tell him how much being with Clara had helped clarify her mind. But she just couldn't. "The time with Clara has been good for me too." But she could never explain why. How could she tell him that being with Clara made her certain that she wanted the joy of having children? She wanted to hug a little girl or a boy every day. No, that was silly and her eyes were filling.

"What is it?" Jurgen put a hand on her shoulder. A pleasing warmth unfurled inside.

She blinked and shook her head. "Nothing. Just thinking about something."

Looking a bit confused, he dropped his hand. "Yes, well…I hope you will come to our suite sometime today. We have a small gift for you. Well, from Clara. And me of course." His cheeks flushed a deeper red, even though the wind had not kicked up. The movement of the ship thrummed against the soles of her feet while her heartbeat went crazy. Surely, he could hear it.

"That would be nice." Where were the words that usually came to her so quickly? In business she was known for her competent presentations. But now words failed her. One look up into his warm brown eyes, and she was at a loss. Turning, she nearly stumbled. But Jurgen quickly reached for her again, holding her in front of him much the way she had held Clara yesterday. His arms bracketed her and she felt the prickle of every hair on his bare forearms. His heart beat rhythmically against her back. Did she feel his lips brush the top of her head? That was crazy. Turning, she found his dark eyes traveling through the ponytail slung over her shoulder as if they were fingers separating each strand. Feeling a bit dizzy, she squeezed her eyes shut.

"Are you all right, Hadley?" His body tensed.

Oh, this was silly and she pried her eyes open. "Yes. Just a little dizzy. Must be lack of food. But I should probably continue my run. My aunt will be getting up soon."

"Yes of course." Then he looked at his arms around her as if he didn't know how they'd gotten there. "But do not stumble, please."

"Then you'll have to let go of me."

Instantly his arms relaxed and he chuckled. "I don't know what's happening to me," he mumbled, digging his right hand into his hair. "I am acting like an idiot."

"Don't tell Clara that. She might believe it."

A rogue breeze tunneled between them. Hadley needed that wake-up call and stepped away. The muscles in her body were twitching, ready to run. "See you later." Turning, she took off. As she ran, the air that had been frigid twenty minutes ago now felt so warm. Or was it her own body that felt feverish? She slapped one hand to her forehead to check. Nothing. Her breath was coming in short white bursts. And it was Christmas. Christmas. She was not at home alone in her condo, thinking about her failed engagement. Yes, that was just what it was and she was very lucky to have realized it.

When she reached the next doorway, she dashed inside to gaze at the Christmas tree in the public area that smelled like pine and the outdoors. One of the cleaning women rushed past carrying a stack of clean towels. They smelled wonderful. Everything was wonderful today. "Merry Christmas," Hadley called out.

"Merry Christmas." The girl gave her a wide smile and hurried away.

The tree rotated on a stand casting its cheerful light into the room. The garland that twirled up the steps had never seemed so green or so bright. The red and green bulbs tucked into the greenery looked so festive. No elevator for her. Hadley dashed up the steps. When she burst into their room, she found Aunt Ethel seated next to the tree in her dressing gown. On the video screen of their artificial fireplace, a fire burned brightly. The tree lights cast a warm glow over the room.

"Merry Christmas!" But no sooner were the words out of Aunt Ethel's lips than her smooth forehead folded into a frown. "Is everything all right? Your face is all red."

"Is it?" Hadley ran to hug her. "I was out running."

"Aren't you the energetic one. I suppose you're hungry?"

"Yes, but first I'd like you to open this gift." Last night Hadley had tucked something under the tree. Now she lifted the lovely green box with the large gold bow and handed it to her aunt. She was pretty sure that Aunt Ethel would like it.

"You shouldn't have gotten me anything, dear. Did you bring this with you?" But her aunt couldn't fool Hadley. She looked pleased and pointed to something under the tree. "That gift is for you."

"Oh, no, Aunt Ethel. Really, you've been too generous." How embarrassing. She couldn't even imagine what this trip was costing her aunt. And then there was that gorgeous gown for New Year's Eve. Without a price tag, who knew what that had cost?

With a fluttering of her fingers, Aunt Ethel waited. "Nonsense. What else do I have to spend my money on? When you're my age, you can only wear so many new clothes."

"Oh, Aunt Ethel. You are too much." The lovely flat box looked as if it had been wrapped at a store. "Why don't we open our gifts together?"

But she waited until her aunt unpeeled the silver paper Hadley had gotten last night from the desk downstairs. She'd collected the demitasse spoons one by one in the different cities while her aunt was busy buying hot chocolate or another pastry. Clara had also provided an excellent diversion. Jurgen too.

"They're beautiful. How did you ever guess?" Her aunt's voice wobbled after she'd lifted the top from the box. Four tiny silver spoons were nested in the tissue paper, each one unique.

"I didn't have to guess. Uncle Oscar gave you demitasse spoons when you traveled. I've seen your collection many times."

"And now I can add these." Aunt Ethel brought the box to her heart. "You dear, sweet girl. Looking at these spoons will always remind me of a truly wonderful Christmas. Now, your turn."

Hadley slid off the silver bow and opened her gift. Maybe a new scarf or some gloves? But no and she gasped at the beautiful necklace displayed on blue velvet. "Oh, this is too much." The sculpted necklace was elegant. The hammered and etched silver came to a point that held a blue stone. "This is much too expensive."

"Nonsense." Her aunt dismissed that idea with a shake of her head. "It was on sale."

Now that made her chuckle. Her aunt had never been known as a bargain hunter. Already Hadley's mind was moving ahead. *Why now, why this?* "New Year's Eve. That wonderful gown. Is that what you were thinking?"

"Yes of course. I'd caught a glimpse of this in a store window near the dress shop. After you settled on the gown, I couldn't get the necklace out of my mind. When I told Elka where it was, she was happy to take care of it for me. A courier brought it late yesterday just before the ship left. Isn't that fun?" Her aunt's delight made her smile. But she did wonder—for about the tenth time on this cruise.

Hadley never had any indication that her aunt lived such a grand life. Couriers. Extravagant suites. Her mother may have known. Mom had always been kind of vague about her aunt and Uncle Oscar. At times she would refer to their trips as "grand adventures." Their city apartment down on Lakeshore Drive had been very nicely done, though.

Aunt Ethel rose with a swish of her dressing gown. "Enough.

The day awaits us." Only her aunt could say something like that and get away with it. But she read all those historical romances. Bringing the gift back to her room, Hadley placed the necklace in her safe. After a quick shower, she dressed and they went down to breakfast.

The Christmas buffet was grander than anything she'd ever seen. While carols played merrily overhead, smiling staff spooned up eggs benedict, tiramisu french toast, or simple scrambled eggs or oatmeal for those who were more health minded. Of course, there were sausages and broiled tomatoes topped with cheese, eggs done three different ways. Omelets made to order, plus pancakes and waffles. Turning to another table, they found spiced apples, eggnog yogurt, curried fruits and pastries galore.

"Look, Hadley. Eggnog french toast. Who would've thought?" Aunt Ethel pointed. She'd already surrendered one plate to a young man in a white coat. Now she took another.

"Maybe I'll come back." Hadley clung to one plate. Seeing that Aunt Ethel was ready, Hadley headed back to their table.

"How absolutely scrumptious. Be sure you taste everything." Aunt Ethel's voice trailed after her. She was turning out to be a very bad influence. "After all, it's Christmas."

The servers were all smiles. Some of the girls wore holly in their hair and the men sported red carnation boutonnieres. They ate slowly, greeting the other travelers as they arrived in the dining room. The atmosphere was upbeat and festive. But Hadley kept looking for Jurgen and Clara.

When her aunt went back for seconds, Hadley followed. They

were finishing up their peppermint coffee when Clara came barreling toward them, the full red velvet skirt of her dress jingling merrily. Her patent leather shoes skidding on the carpet, Clara came to a halt with Jurgen right behind. Hadley opened her arms for a big hug and the little girl tumbled into them.

"And what princess do we have here?" Hadley teased.

"How did you know?"

"Hadley thinks you must be one of the fairies, like in *The Nutcracker Suite*," Jurgen explained. The little girl's dress was a wonder. A white lace collar set off the fitted bodice embroidered with sprigs of holly. The floor-length skirt hid the jingle bells, keeping Clara in continual motion.

"Today everyone will hear you coming, Clara," Hadley teased.

Throwing out her arms, Clara trumpeted, "I know!"

But Clara was not the only one who caught Hadley's attention. Jurgen wore a green velvet jacket piped in gold. And if any of the women on board had not noticed him earlier, certainly Christmas would change that. A crisp white shirt was emphasized by an ascot embroidered with holly berries. This morning the sun falling in the side windows gave his brown eyes a greenish cast. Not that she noticed. Blushing, Hadley turned away.

"My goodness," her aunt murmured with appreciation. "Jurgen is quite the man."

Without thinking, Hadley nodded. "Yes, yes he is."

Had he heard her? Were his cheeks flushing from her comment? Turning, she grabbed the syrup and proceeded to drown her eggnog french toast. "Have a bite?" she asked Clara, cutting off a tiny piece. To her surprise, Clara opened her lips like a little bird. Hadley popped in the rich morsel.

The pleased smile on Clara's face was the best Christmas present Hadley could ever have. Glancing up she met Jurgen's eyes. He was smiling, as if they were sharing this special moment, just the two of them.

"You'll find that and more on the buffet." Hadley made herself look away.

"Yes, well, again Merry Christmas." Was that all Jurgen could say?

"Please come to our suite around two o'clock." As he turned to leave, Jurgen gently put a hand on her shoulder. "I mean, if that's convenient."

"We have a present for you," Clara added, her eyes sparkling.

"But of course." Her aunt exchanged a look with Hadley. "We'll see you then."

Jurgen and Clara moved on. Reaching up, Hadley touched her shoulder, which still tingled. Her aunt looked so pleased.

"What?" Hadley dropped her hand.

"Oh nothing." Her aunt glanced away. "I wonder what Jurgen has for you."

"*Us*," Hadley emphasized, pushing back her chair as one of the waiters rushed to help her. "He said he had a gift for *us*."

"If you say so." Aunt Ethel could be so funny.

Leaving the main dining room, they greeted people who had joined them on excursions. Friends for a week, they had played cornhole or darts together. Or simply nodded to each other on the bus. For this special day, everyone was great friends.

"I think I need a nap," Hadley said when they reached the room. She'd gotten up so early to run. "I shouldn't have eaten all that french toast."

Aunt Ethel yawned. "I'll do the same. We have to meet Jurgen at two and it's already past noon."

"And I want to write to Brock." Just saying his name, her happy mood evaporated, leaving only a nervous tremor in her stomach.

"Have you heard much from him?" Her aunt paused at the door to her room.

"Off and on." What could she say? "Want to call Mom and Dad?"

"Great idea." For a few minutes, their naps and Brock were forgotten. The call was chaotic, coming in and out.

"And how is the trip?" her mother asked. "Leanne and Mindy have been sharing your posts. My goodness you've been busy."

"They print up a schedule every day."

"We're hardly ever in the room," Aunt Ethel said over Hadley's shoulder.

"And you're both having fun?"

"You bet." Hadley smiled up at her aunt.

"Any word from you know who?"

Brock. Not very subtle and Hadley hated the fact that her mother was still hoping. "Not much and I'm okay with that."

"She's been much too busy to miss him," her aunt threw in.

The call ended and they both disappeared into their rooms.

When she flipped open her laptop, Hadley found no new email

from Brock. But he'd never been an early riser and Chicago was six or seven hours behind her. Still she sent off a quick "Merry Christmas. Have a wonderful day." And then her finger stalled. Was he going to be with his family today? He hadn't revealed any of his plans.

She glanced at her finger. What did this ring mean, anyway?

Her engagement ring felt so heavy. Although she'd caught her aunt looking at the ring, Aunt Ethel had never questioned her about her plans. Hadley felt relieved because at that point, she didn't have any answers. But she knew how she felt.

Now she slipped the ring off and tucked it into the safe next to her beautiful new necklace. Usually she made important decisions quickly. This one had taken longer but it felt oh, so right.

Chapter 17

Hadley had trouble getting dressed later that afternoon. Why was she so excited? This was ridiculous. Looking back, this trip had turned out to be so different from what she'd expected. She'd pictured shopping a lot with her aunt. And of course Hadley would be her companion at dinner. But she's also expected some communications from Brock. Something to show her where his head was. After all, she'd promised him that she would think over his concern about their family plans. After this time away from him, she saw their conversation in a different light. The more she thought about it, the angrier she got. Aunt Ethel had been right. Brock hadn't been totally honest with her. Somehow she knew that.

Over the past few days, she'd spent time wondering about her own future. Every time she got an email from Miranda, she felt her stressful career roll over on her in a crushing wave. As the days passed, she dreaded going back.

"You look lovely," she told her aunt when they met in the salon to go to Jurgen's. The red tunic top was very flattering and showcased her gold jewelry, understated today and very tasteful.

"So do you. That green sweater is fabulous with your blonde hair." The sweater was patterned with snowflakes stitched in gold, one of Hadley's impulse buys on that shopping trip that felt so long ago. With it, she was wearing her winter white slacks and white boots.

Together, they had collaborated on a gift for Jurgen and Clara. Something the father and daughter would have as a memory of this trip. Would they look back on this cruise in years to come and think of the two Americans who had shared so much time with them? She hoped they hadn't monopolized Jurgen and Clara. But she'd never noticed them teaming up with any of the other guests. Once they returned to their home in Starengard, wherever that was, they would pick up their lives. Christmas would become just a memory. Going over to the tree, she picked up an extra box she'd wrapped the night before.

"What do you have there?" her aunt asked.

"Just a little something for Clara. Online shopping is amazing. I'm so glad that they can deliver to the ship." Pocketing the keycard, Hadley ushered her aunt out of the suite.

Clara opened the door at the first knock. "Merry Christmas!" Hadley greeted her.

"Merry Christmas!" Clara said with such excitement in her voice. You would have thought that they hadn't seen each other for a long time. The little girl was still in her red Christmas dress. Giggling, she danced over to a massive tree filled with ornaments and white lights while Shatzi nipped at her heels. The color scheme was green and silver with wide silver ribbons cascading down the tree from a bright star. Watching Clara twirl around, Hadley could hardly believe this was the same little girl she'd disturbed in the laundry just over a week ago. She gave Clara the box to put under the tree and laughed when the little girl gave it a good shake.

"Oh my." Aunt Ethel was taking in the tree that looked much larger than the one in their suite. Hadley hoped her aunt wouldn't mind. Jurgen gave Aunt Ethel a polite kiss on both cheeks—very European—while Hadley studied the tree. She wondered about some of the ornaments that had what looked like a coat of arms. When she turned, Jurgen was there. When her aunt went to give Clara a hug, Hadley stood waiting and wondering. What should she do? He came closer.

"Merry Christmas, Jurgen."

"Merry Christmas. Once again." They laughed. The morning felt so long ago. Hands gently cupping her elbows, Jurgen gave her a soft kiss on each cheek. The subtle brush of faint chin stubble sent warmth catapulting through her body. She felt shaken and he looked surprised but pleased and so very handsome in that velvet jacket. Somehow he'd ended up with lipstick on his left cheek. When she moved to brush it off, Hadley couldn't even look at him. Jurgen caught her hand in his for just a second before they broke apart with a soft smile.

Her aunt came to her rescue, holding up their gift. "And here is a small something from Hadley and me. A little memento of the trip."

"Oh, I love presents! Papa, may I open it?" Clara was not to be left out.

"Yes, of course but first let's all sit down." And he motioned to the comfortable chairs and sofa. Aunt Ethel took one of the chairs with a very solid back and Hadley sat in the other.

Jurgen and Clara shared the sofa. By that time Clara had confiscated the gift. "I'll do it, Papa."

In the corner was a mirrored bar. While the four of them were busy with the gifts, Emerson and Miss Schmidt had been putting together a platter of what looked like warmed quiche. The smell of eggnog was in the air and Emerson was sprinkling nutmeg on the foamy contents of the punch bowl.

Within seconds, Clara had the gift open. "Pictures, Papa." And Hadley couldn't tell if she was a bit disappointed. Maybe this was like getting clothes for Christmas when she was a little girl. She'd always hated that, and her brother and sister felt the same. But Jurgen didn't look disappointed at all.

"Let's see." Jurgen carefully opened the three-panel frame.

To Hadley's relief, they both look delighted when they saw the pictures inside. "How wonderful," Jurgen said. "We will cherish these always."

Hadley had taken several pictures of Clara and Jurgen. But the one on the right was an unauthorized substitution. She gave her aunt a questioning glance. Aunt Ethel looked away, accepting a glass of eggnog from Emerson.

In one picture Jurgen and his little girl were playing cornhole, their expressions hopeful although Clara looked frustrated. Priceless, really. Hadley was so grateful that she'd gotten that candid shot. In the center picture, Jurgen and Clara were shopping for the marionette. What could have been better? The shot captured Clara's excitement and the busy market perfectly as the shopkeeper showed them how to work the puppets.

But in the third picture——the unauthorized one—Hadley ice-skated behind Clara. Jurgen had just joined them and the three of them huddled together. But her aunt had caught Jurgen and Clara smiling at Hadley. She wouldn't even try to interpret those smiles.

"We will cherish this always," Jurgen said, taking the gift from Clara's hands. "Thank you. Both of you. You have made this trip something I could never have envisioned."

Was he all choked up? Jurgen? While Miss Schmidt handed her a glass of eggnog, Jurgen set the pictures up on the mantel.

"I want to go skating again, Papa. Can I?" Clara asked, dancing up and down. She had so much energy.

"When we get home, I'm sure Miss Schmidt can make arrangements for you to go skating."

Well, Hadley almost hooted at that one. The very thought of the stern Miss Schmidt arranging ice-skating was hilarious. Would she attempt it herself? That could be dangerous.

"And Hadley too, right?" Clara followed her father back to the sofa.

Aunt Ethel was suddenly very busy with her small clutch bag.

"We'll see, Clara," her father said. Now, what did that mean?

"One more thing." Hadley had almost forgotten. "Clara, that box wrapped in green foil is for you."

"For me?" After grabbing the box, Clara sat down on the floor and stripped off the paper. When she flicked the top off the box, her mouth dropped open. "Red cowboy boots!"

"How did you know the size?" Jurgen asked. Clara was already kicking off her patent leather shoes. Hadley was relieved to see that the boots fit. Jumping up, Clara lifted her skirts so her new boots were visible.

"Miss Schmidt helped me." Hadley had cornered her one day but it hadn't been easy. Still busy with the quiche, Clara's nanny blushed furiously.

To Hadley's amazement, Clara threw herself into her arms. "I love you, Hadley! You're the best." Lifting her face, Clara smiled up at her. Then she broke away and danced toward the tree. Shatzi was going crazy.

What could Hadley say? "You too, sweetheart. The very best." But her voice was choked, a mere whisper. Aunt Ethel reached over to squeeze her hand.

Looking stunned himself, Jurgen settled himself on the sofa as if he was going to make an announcement. "I have a gift for all of you." His eyes circled the room, including Emerson and Miss Schmidt.

"What is it, Papa? Is this something for me too?" Clearly Clara had eaten too much sugar that morning. She could not sit down. Her jingle bells rang merrily as she stomped about in her new boots.

"Tomorrow we leave for Vienna and I've arranged tickets for us to see *The Nutcracker*!" He looked so pleased. Hadley could hardly believe his announcement. Certainly those holiday tickets had been snapped up before now.

"*The Nutcracker?*" Clara was trying to get her mind around that. "You mean where pretty girls dance and wear beautiful clothes?"

"Exactly. Like in the poster."

"Papa! You make me so happy!" She threw herself at her father.

Smiling, Jurgen looked pleased by his little girl's excitement. Hadley was beside herself with excitement. "How wonderful to see that ballet in Vienna." She would remember this performance all her life.

"Indeed, and I think the ballet is playing in Vienna's opera house." Something about Aunt Ethel's tone made Hadley turn.

"Yes, a beautiful building which will only enhance the performance, I'm sure." Was Jurgen being evasive? "Of course Emerson and Miss Schmidt will join us. As they have throughout the trip."

That was partially true. As the days had gone by, the two seemed to draw into themselves and their own activities. Jurgen didn't seem to mind.

But Aunt Ethel was not finished. The woman could be a stickler for details. "I would think that those tickets sold out months ago. May I ask, how are you so fortunate?"

"A friend of mine has a box and he's not using his tickets." Hands on his knees, Jurgen was very matter-of-fact about it.

"How very convenient. And lucky."

"We're lucky. Right, Papa?" Clara chimed in.

Sitting together in the salon, Hadley felt both excited and a bit sad. She couldn't wait to see Vienna. The city had always been one of Aunt Ethel's favorites, so she'd heard plenty about it. But the trip was winding down, and Hadley didn't feel ready to leave the ship. She had made so many happy memories here.

As they sat there talking about their plans, they nibbled quiche and sipped eggnog. The drapes were open so they could enjoy the scenery as the boat moved along. They stayed about an hour and then left. Aunt Ethel quickly disappeared into her room.

Leaving the door to the salon open so that she could enjoy the tree, Hadley relaxed in her room and checked her emails. Nothing from Brock. Really, what else was there to say? She didn't want to ruin his holiday.

Christmas caroling had been scheduled for later in the afternoon. So around four thirty they bundled up and went to the top deck. Some of the staff were dressed in red gowns with white collars. What fun they seem to have singing favorite carols from several countries. When it came to "O Tannenbaum," everyone joined in, their languages intertwining.

As their voices lifted, the music was so beautiful. Their countries might sometimes have differences, but that day they were all united and celebrating the holiday. Although she'd dreaded this day, Hadley was sad to see it slip away. Darkness came early at this time of year. While they sang, strings of lights glowed over the carolers and the guests, now cuddled in blankets. Jurgen and Clara never appeared and she felt disappointed.

Aunt Ethel wanted to have a light dinner served in their suite. Hadley agreed and was happy when small sandwiches and a fruit plate arrived. Together they watched "It's a Wonderful Life" on the private TV channel. The movie was a perfect end to their day.

After kissing Aunt Ethel good night, Hadley went into her own room and pulled up her email again. When she saw Brock's message, she felt a ripple of anxiety. Why was she so riddled with uncertainty? After their lunch a couple of weeks ago and the few short emails she received, Hadley didn't know what to expect.

"Merry Christmas, my love," his text read. *My love?* Where did that come from? This didn't even sound like him. Hadley kept reading. "I have many surprises for you. I've decided to go into business on my own. Isn't that exciting? Something I've always wanted to do."

She looked up. Her drapes were still open. Outside, snow was falling softly on the water. When had he mentioned opening his own business? The scene outside was so peaceful, but reading this message, she didn't feel peaceful at all. Her eyes fell back to the screen.

"From your Facebook posts, I guess you'll be going to Vienna. Thought I might fly and meet you there. What do you think? Won't that be exciting? I've been thinking about everything you said. I have to admit that I can't live without you. So please consider this and get back to me. Brock"

Who is this man? She fell back in her chair. The message was so confusing. He'd never mentioned a job change in his future. And what did he mean that he would meet them in Vienna? Was he planning on joining them for the remainder of the cruise? She didn't see how that would be possible. Staring at her laptop, she felt riddled with frustration. The carpet felt cold on her bare feet as she walked to the windows and pushed the button to close the drapes.

Brock couldn't come. That wouldn't work at all. And most of

all, she didn't want him to come. She began to type. "Dear Brock, you were so right that day at lunch. There was so much we didn't know about each other. But now I realize we should go our separate ways. I wish you well. Hadley"

As she got ready for bed, Hadley knew that she'd changed. What she'd wanted almost two weeks ago might not be what she wanted now. But then, what did she see in her future? She wasn't sure of anything but she knew her life was starting to take a new course.

Chapter 18

Hadley could hardly move. Her body felt heavy and her mind was in a fog. Vienna was only a day away and today was a free day on the ship. But she had absolutely no energy. Running in the early morning felt lonely and drab. The weather had turned harshly cold. The clouds scooting across the still, dark sky might mean more snow. Back in the salon, she asked Aunt Ethel to go to breakfast without her.

"You don't mind, do you?" she asked her aunt.

"Not at all. You know me. Social butterfly."

Hadley loved her aunt's independence. But after she left the suite, the rooms seemed too quiet. Too empty. When she thought she heard Shatzi, barking beyond their wall, she was tempted to go over there. Knock on their door. But of course that was ridiculous. She couldn't barge in on Jurgen and Clara. What excuse would she give?

Had Christmas worn her out? Or was it all the thinking and analyzing she had to do about herself? Brock kept pestering her after her last message that told him not to come. He wouldn't give up. Wanted a reason. But she didn't want to go into it and didn't know what to say.

When the ship offered a trip to Krems, she decided to stay behind. And so did her aunt. "I hope you're feeling all right?" Hadley said. The two of them were stretched out on chairs up on the top deck. The clouds had cleared and they were cuddled under one of the soft blue snowflake blankets.

"I'm feeling fine. Isn't this delightful?" Looking lazy and content, her aunt looked over at her. A small part of Hadley felt jealous. Someday she wanted to be a lady of leisure like her aunt. "I do believe this is the best cruise I've ever taken. Well of course with the exception of…"

"Yes, I understand. Uncle Oscar." No cruise could ever take the place of the ones that her great aunt had shared with her uncle. Hadley understood that.

"That said, this has been quite an active cruise. I think you and that little Clara have worn me out." But she didn't seem disappointed at all.

"She's a darling little girl." Hadley felt happy thinking about Clara with the long blonde hair. "If only Jurgen would learn how to take care of her hair."

Her aunt chuckled gleefully. "I believe that is Miss Schmidt's duty, not that she would look at it like that."

"Probably not. I can't understand why Jurgen has that older woman in charge of Clara. She's such a buzz kill."

"Not sure what that means, dear, but I quite agree."

"Clara has so much spirit. I'm afraid Miss Schmidt will squelch all that."

"Maybe you should have been an elementary school teacher,

Hadley." Aunt Ethel rearranged her blanket. "Emerson has indicated that Miss Schmidt might be on her way out."

Now that was astonishing. "Really? But my impression is that she's been with the family forever."

"Exactly. And that's the problem. Emerson himself is nearing retirement."

Turning, Hadley studied her aunt. Where was she getting all this information? "Jurgen has mentioned his mother but not much about her. Maybe Clara's grandmother will take her in hand."

"Maybe." But her aunt didn't sound convinced. "And what about your young man? Did you ever hear from him on Christmas Day?"

Hadley was surprised that it had taken her aunt so long to ask. Glancing down at her bare ring finger, she knew that her aunt had noticed.

"Yes, Brock emailed me on Christmas. But he didn't like what I had to say." Briefly she brought her aunt up to speed. "I told Brock there was no reason for him to come."

"A difficult choice for you, I'm sure."

"Choice? I suppose it is. When I think of all of the planning that's gone into our wedding, I feel terrible. My poor parents. What will they think?"

"Your parents want you to be happy. Certainly reconsidering that relationship is worth the investment rather than making a mistake you'll regret. A marriage is a key decision, Hadley."

"For such a long time I thought Brock was the man for me. Only a year ago we both made the list of Chicago's Young Movers and Shakers. Both hard working up-and-comers. Maybe that's what kept us together."

Her aunt raised her delicate eyebrows. "Yes, but a marriage is more than a business arrangement."

"I know." They were seated toward the back of the ship. Under the gray sky the Danube itself looked bluish gray today as it wound its way around the docked ship. Hadley rubbed her forehead. "I wish things felt more clear for me. After Brock, I really question my own judgment. Why did I think he was so perfect for me? Maybe I took so much for granted when I assumed that we were on the same page about having a family."

"Don't blame yourself, Hadley. I think your young man's silence on that point probably was taken as agreement. He could have clarified that at any time. My guess is, he chose not to."

"Could be." Overhead, the sun was trying to break through the clouds, sending slivers of light over the water. "We were always so busy. My job is crazy. I don't know what I'm going to do about that. And Brock's work puts him under a lot of pressure."

"And from what I understand his company is having some problems."

She turned to face her aunt. "Really? Where did you hear that?"

"In the papers. Isn't his firm Sterling, Welsh and Long?"

"Yes." Hadley could barely breathe.

"They're going through major layoffs, according to the *Tribune*." Aunt Ethel shot Hadley a crooked smile. "Do you think that had anything to do with Brock's sudden urge to reunite with you in Vienna?"

Disappointment swept over her, followed by anger. "Wow. Maybe. That stinker." Some of the pieces fell into place and Hadley wanted to strangle him.

Looking out over the water, her aunt nodded. "Indeed. When we're young, I think we envision our perfect life. Wonderful house, expensive cars, handsome husband…all that. But that doesn't mean it's the *best* life we could have. The life we could have if we were that brave."

"Brave?" What was her aunt saying?

But Aunt Ethel had gone back to fussing with her blanket. Strictly a diversionary tactic. Then she brought her attention back to Hadley. "Soon all things will be clear regarding Brock. Seems to me you have to get on with your life. Won't you miss some of the people you've met on this cruise?"

"Oh yes. Of course. Clara…" Her throat closed. That little mischief and her darling Shatzi.

"Life takes tremendous bravery," her aunt continued. "That is, if you really live it." Her eyes sparkled as she looked out at the shoreline where bushes were strung with lights and candles glowed in every window.

"I don't want to go back to work."

"But I thought you loved your job."

"I did too. Things have changed, including the way I feel about my career." What had it gotten her? A beautiful condo she never had time to enjoy. A life that had been put on hold. "I've lived more in the past week and a half than I have in the past two or three years. Relaxed more and had fun."

"Maybe you should listen to that feeling."

Her entire body felt heavy every time Hadley thought about going back. "But the ship isn't real, is it?"

"I guess that's the question."

Hadley had no idea what her aunt meant.

***

The following day when they woke up, the ship had docked at Vienna. Hadley and her aunt ate breakfast quickly because the shore excursion bus was leaving early. When they approached the buses lined up in the parking lot up near the ship, they found Jurgen and Clara waiting for them. Clara was wearing her torn jeans and they weren't even fighting about it. On her feet were the red cowboy boots. She looked darling.

"Oh, my goodness," Aunt Ethel said, sounding very pleased. "Are you waiting for us?"

"We most certainly are." Jurgen looked a little shame-faced. "And we hope that that's all right with you." His eyes went to Hadley.

"Yes of course." Her spirits lifted as she climbed onboard with Clara chattering right behind her.

"We match," the little girl murmured against Hadley's back.

"We sure do." They were both wearing red sweaters with their torn jeans, jackets and red boots. When Hadley took a seat, Clara quickly filed in right behind her. That left Aunt Ethel and Jurgen in the seats in front of them. Hadley could keep an eye on them. The two of them talking together alone? That could be a dangerous combination.

The day proved to be a whirlwind tour of Vienna, from the old Viennese Christmas market to the Belvedere Palace. Since they had shopped rigorously in Prague and Cologne, and because Christmas was over, there was nothing Hadley wanted to buy. Aunt Ethel seemed to feel the same way. But there was still so much to see.

Although she'd heard of the Lipizzaner stallions—they'd even come to Chicago once or twice—she'd never seen them perform. Jurgen had arranged a private tour.

"Traveling with Jurgen is certainly first class," her aunt whispered as they entered the riding school. The rich smell of horses and sawdust was not unpleasant. Stepping over to one of the gentlemen in livery, Jurgen had a conversation. Their guide appeared immediately. First they went through the stables for an inside peek as he filled them in with more information about breeding the stallions than she could ever remember.

This training area was only for the best of the colts, they learned. The stalls and paths were very neatly kept, overlaid with the rich smell of leather and horses. But when their guide mentioned separating the colts from their mothers after two years, Clara's excitement cooled. The sorrow on her face tugged at Haley's heart.

"But what happens, Papa, when they take the baby horses from their mothers?" That part didn't sit well with Clara. Hadley didn't blame her.

Stooping, Jurgen took her hands. "Don't worry, sweetheart. The horses have a good life. After two years with their mothers, they are ready to be trained."

"Like our horses?" Clara asked, tears trembling in her voice. She was so sensitive. Given her history, Hadley could totally understand that.

But Hadley was curious about the horses that Jurgen apparently owned.

"Yes," Jurgen said quietly. "Like our horses. Maybe even better."

By that time they were on their way up to a viewing balcony. As they filed into the red velvet seats, Hadley turned to Jurgen. She couldn't let this pass. Maybe she was learning her technique from her aunt. "So you have horses?" He had said so little about his home or his village—wherever he lived. She didn't want to pry but she was curious.

"Oh yes. Very common over here." But he avoided her eyes.

Now, what did that mean? Where was "over here?" Her aunt had heard Hadley's question. They would probably talk about this later. Her attention went back to the stadium where the horses had entered led by their trainers. Classical music played as trainers put the horses through some exercises. These horses were truly amazing.

Just when she thought it couldn't get any better, the trainer brought out one of the mature stallions. Muscles rippling under his shiny coat, the stallion captured their attention. The short performance began and the horse's training was evident in his amazing leaps.

At the end, Clara leapt to her feet, applauding. "Papa, the horse is dancing!"

Looking over his daughter's head, Jurgen smiled at Hadley. "Yes, sweetheart, he is trained to dance."

Dropping a hand onto her father's shoulder, Clara became very serious. "Can Mahler teach our horses to dance?"

But Jurgen shook his head. "No, you need a special kind of horse with a muscular structure. Our horses cannot dance. These horses are bred for it."

Subdued, Clara sat down and they went back to enjoying the exhibit. Soon after that, they left.

Walking back to the bus, Aunt Ethel took Clara's hand and walked ahead of them, which left Hadley and Jurgen. "Thank you for today," she said, the winter sunlight warm on her shoulders. "I feel as if I've gotten an inside look."

"I'm glad you enjoyed it. The stallions are a long-standing tradition for the Viennese."

"So, tell me more about your own horses." Aunt Ethel and Clara had moved ahead of them. Sometimes her aunt could surprise Hadley with her speed.

"Our horses are not all stallions like these, although we do show some of them. Do you ride?"

"Oh no. This life is very different from mine," she said with a sigh. "I live in the city."

Jurgen looked almost disappointed. "Have you ever wanted to learn how to ride? You seem to be quite athletic."

"Maybe. But my work keeps me busy. Far away from this type of life, unfortunately." From what she'd seen during their excursions, here it was easy to find yourself in the country within twenty minutes or so. But living in downtown Chicago, it might take an hour to reach the outskirts. And she imagined that the cost of riding at a stable would be prohibitive.

But Jurgen was chuckling. "Says the woman who likes adventure."

Since they'd reached the bus, Hadley had no time to respond. But Jurgen seemed to be echoing some of what Aunt Ethel had talked about that morning. Was a different life impossible? Maybe. It would take such effort.

"How did your family like that tour?" the bus driver asked as the four of them climbed on board the bus.

"Oh, we are not…" Hadley began before Jurgen came up close behind her.

"Very well, thank you." Jurgen's hand was on Hadley's back and she kept moving. He could be very old fashioned, opening doors for her and shepherding them through crowds. She was surprised by how much she was enjoying that.

After they found seats together, Hadley happened to glance out the window. Earlier, she thought she'd seen the two men in black from the corner of her eyes. But when she searched for them, they weren't there. She must have been imagining things.

Now she tried to relax into her seat. Once the bus was filled, they left the historical district. They had already made the decision that they wouldn't spend time in the opera house since they would be there for the ballet. Next stop was Belvedere Palace and the bus climbed a small hill to get there. The only thing she knew about this palace was that it housed some of Gustav Klimt's most important works. She loved that artist.

"I've been here before," her aunt told her, breaking away from the group once they'd left the bus. Hadley was beginning to realize that her aunt liked to do things her own way. Being with the group was not always to her taste. Once inside the impressive stone structure, Aunt Ethel climbed the stairs with amazing speed and grace, the three of them right behind her.

"Do you know Klimt's work?" Jurgen asked as they entered the gallery.

"Yes," her aunt answered, huffing a little when they reached the second floor. "Why don't I take Clara to see Monet? She might like his work better." And with that Aunt Ethel hustled off, with Clara tossing them a backward glance. Hadley secretly thought the little girl enjoyed the private attention. She knew how that had felt when she was about Clara's age. Her aunt and uncle had taken her to the Art Museum in downtown Chicago. Trips like that had been one of the benefits of being the oldest child.

"Does your aunt believe Klimt's work is for adults?" Jurgen watched them leave.

"Your guess is as good as mine. But she does enjoy being with Clara. She was always very attentive to me when I was growing up. I was the oldest. Maybe she experimented on me."

"Doesn't she have grandchildren of her own?"

"Sadly no. That was not in the cards for them." By this time they were standing in front of the famous painting "The Kiss." It was impossible not to be moved.

"Powerful, yes?" Jurgen said.

"Yes, very." Words failed her. Taking in their embrace, Hadley knew she had never been kissed like this. And she also knew that her decision about Brock had been the right one.

"Are you crying?" Jurgen's concerned expression made her blink and turn away. She didn't want anyone to see her like this. How foolish. And she gently ran her fingers under both eyes.

"Why such tears?" Others were arriving and Jurgen led her into one of the deep windows.

Looking up at him, she managed a watery smile. "Maybe deep emotions like this are just for paintings, right?"

"Not at all. Not when love is right."

The windows overlooked the terraced garden and the view was spectacular. Avoiding his gaze, she concentrated on the hillside. When was love "right," as he'd just said?

"Forgive me, but I noticed that you no longer wear your ring."

Fanning out the bare fingers of her left hand, Hadley nodded. "Yes, I came to a decision. And it's the right one for me." She'd been sleeping better, although she wasn't going to tell him that.

"I'm so glad. Sorry to be so bold but…" His discomfort made her smile. Jurgen always took two steps forward and one step back. She was beginning to wonder about that.

But just as this conversation was becoming interesting, Clara charged toward them, her cowboy boots clattering on the parquet floors. Other visitors turned to smile at the little girl in the red coat and boots. Hadley wished Miss Schmidt would master the french braids or even a decent ponytail. But no, Clara's hair flew wildly about her. "Papa, Aunt Ethel showed me beautiful flowers. Almost like the ones in our garden."

"You must show me." But as he was pulled away, Jurgen sent Hadley a backward glance that made her wonder what he'd been about to say. A look that stirred her more than any kiss she'd ever experienced.

Chapter 19

When Hadley woke up, late the following morning, Aunt Ethel was gone. Over the last couple of days, her aunt had become more independent. Sometimes she would leave a note that she was out walking. Walking? Aunt Ethel? Hadley couldn't figure that out.

Changing into her workout clothes, Hadley went down to the fitness center. She walked on the treadmill, set to the appropriate tilt. Smiling, she thought back to that first day with Jurgen on the treadmill next to her. They'd been strangers. He'd been horrified by her, which irritated her no end. Sometimes she felt that she still took him by surprise. And she enjoyed those moments.

Now that she knew Jurgen and Clara pretty well, she'd miss them when the cruise was over. Maybe that was one of the drawbacks to these trips. Had Aunt Ethel ever met people that she hoped to see again? Every time Clara found her in the dining room or up on the deck, the little girl just about turned inside out.

How did Aunt Ethel handle this? Of course, when Uncle Oscar was on the scene, that was different. But she'd taken up traveling alone or with a group after her uncle was gone. She didn't remember her mother mentioning that Aunt Ethel had befriended anyone on one of her trips. Maybe it was foolish to form a close relationship while traveling. In Chicago, she didn't have a lot of time to develop friendships. Sure, she might meet someone for a drink after work. But then she had to move on. There was always something she had to do. Increasing the speed of the treadmill, she gripped the handrails and tried to clear her mind.

Back in the room, she quickly showered and changed. By that time she was starving. Her appetite had increased quite a bit. It would be hard to go back to having only coffee and oatmeal in the morning. As much as she talked about the other dining options with her aunt, they both gravitated towards the main dining room. Maybe it was the formality of the room with the linen tablecloth and flowers on the table, but they both liked it.

When she reached the main dining room, she went straight for the buffet. Before long, she'd be back on a diet so she had no qualms about having the Belgian waffles today. Strawberries and whipped cream? Bring them on. As she walked toward an empty table by the window, she stopped in her tracks. Was that Aunt Ethel getting up from a table with Emerson? They were both laughing and her aunt had a certain glow. Sitting down quickly, Hadley buried her head in a menu she didn't need to read. What was going on? She had to think about this.

"Coffee ma'am?" The waiter startled her but she managed to nod. By the time she got her bearings again, her aunt was gone. How fascinating. She poured warm syrup over the waffles.

"Hadley, Hadley!" With Jurgen trailing behind her, Clara ran toward her. How could Hadley ever have contemplated a life without children? Someday she hoped to see this excited expectation on the faces of her own children. But today she had Clara.

"The waffles are wonderful. Want a bite?" She loved to tease the little girl with food. And yesterday she'd noticed that she was eating more than cinnamon toast for breakfast.

"I want some of my own, Papa. Please?"

Barely hiding his surprise, Jurgen went off to fill their plates. She loved watching him move. With his back straight, Jurgen had a certain bearing. Now Hadley was being just plain foolish and she ducked her head.

"What are we going to do today?" Clara asked.

"Aunt Ethel and I have booked a day at the spa." Looking over the menu of amenities on the ship, she'd decided she didn't want to leave until she took full advantage of them. "I want to look pretty tonight for the ballet."

Clara's lower lip came out. "Well, I want to look pretty too. Like the ballerinas, right?"

Now that made Hadley laugh. This was so Clara. She didn't want to be outdone. "Trust me, I will not look like the ballerinas. But I want to look my best." She fluttered her fingers in front of her. "And I need a manicure."

Clara was studying Hadley's fingers very seriously when Jurgen returned. "Papa, can I go to the spa with Hadley today?"

Thank goodness Jurgen had already set the two plates on the table or he might have dropped them. "Well, I..."

"It's fine with me," Hadley hastened to say. "And Aunt Ethel will enjoy the company. We'll have a girls' day." And after seeing her aunt with Emerson, she didn't know what to think. Would her aunt have other plans today?

"A girls' day." Clara looked mystified and thrilled.

"You're sure this is all right with you?" Jurgen may have no clue what a girls' day was.

"More than okay." Picking up a fork, Hadley went back to eating. She smiled as Clara took her first bite of the waffle. Clara was so preoccupied as they talked about the spa and what it would entail that she finished her waffle almost before she realized what she was eating.

"Hmm. That was pretty good." She stared down at her empty plate.

Two hours later, Hadley was stretched out having a massage. Her aunt lay on another table nearby. Clara was having her hair shampooed. "Traveling with you is sure a lot of fun," her aunt said as a woman named Mira worked on her back. They were both settled on their stomachs.

"This has been a dream trip, Aunt Ethel." Hadley had told her aunt that so many times but still, it would never be enough. "This Christmas break will stay with me for a long, long time."

"Oh, I'm sure it will." They both had towels wrapped around their heads.

"Lorelei, I wish I could take you back to Chicago with me." This type of deep relaxation was something Hadley never had time for.

The young girl giggled. "Madam, I wish I could go with you to the big city. I have never been there."

"Trust me, it's a great place. But my crazy schedule doesn't leave me many days like this." She shared a smile with her aunt.

"Life is short," her aunt said as the two massage therapists laid the hot stones along their spines.

"You keep saying that." But Hadley didn't want to think about that today.

After the massages, they met Clara at the pool. Each of them had been given a cruise bathing suit in a wonderful shade of turquoise with the white emblem above the legs. While her aunt enjoyed the jacuzzi, Hadley taught Clara how to do a back float in the pool.

"Do you do much swimming at home?" She felt a little guilty about pumping Clara for information but why not?

"In the summer we do. Papa likes to swim. But not in the winter so much. Miss Schmidt does not like to swim and she does not like our indoor pool."

For a fleeting moment, Hadley imagined Jurgen in a bathing suit. She had to swallow hard and concentrate on keeping Clara's arms out to her side. "Y-you have an indoor pool?"

"Yes, but it is not as nice as this one."

"Asking questions, are we?" Aunt Ethel said slyly from the corner Jacuzzi.

Maybe it was time to get out of the pool. Wrapped in the soft terrycloth robes, the three of them stretched out on the chaise lounges for their facials. The women had assured Hadley that they would use something very mild on Clara's skin. When it was time to place fresh cucumber slices on their eyes, the little girl giggled.

"Do you think I'm a salad, Hadley?"

"You don't have circles under your eyes, Clara. So you probably don't need these cucumbers." But Hadley knew what the response would be.

"Oh no, I want the cucumbers. Can you take a picture for Papa?" And Clara sat up in her chair. Although the robe was child size, she still looked lost in it.

"Fine." One of the women handed Hadley her purse so she could fetch her phone. "These pictures are definitely not going on Facebook, Aunt Ethel, so no worries there."

The women must offer to take pictures a lot because Maria was good at it. "Thank you," Hadley said, setting her phone on the table beside her.

While they sat there, the ladies served cool glasses of water with lemon for hydration. Then they switched to hot mulled wine for Aunt Ethel and Hadley, while Clara sipped warm apple juice. Lunch consisted of delicate strips of wheat bread layered with the cucumbers and tuna, clusters of red grapes and applesauce that did not come in a jar. Although Clara at first questioned the sandwiches, they must have passed muster because she ate.

Probably the most fun for Clara was the manicure. When Hadley chose red nail polish with a sprig of holly on each nail, Aunt Ethel decided on the same. But Clara wanted tiny Christmas trees. The salon offered a lot of design choices, among them a holiday tree. Clara could hardly contain herself as her nail tech worked. While their nails were drying, they were ushered over to the black marble shampoo bowls. Aunt Ethel and Hadley were shampooed while a stylist began to blow dry Clara's hair, adding some soft curls.

"Tired?" Hadley asked Clara when she studied the little girl's hair. The curls fell to her shoulders.

The little girl shook her head very seriously. "Nope." Hadley caught Aunt Ethel's smile. This girls' day had turned into a huge hit. And she wondered what Jurgen would think of Clara's new look.

Chapter 20

The stonework of the buildings in Vienna's historical district was beautiful. But nothing had prepared Hadley for the elegance of the opera house. The Vienna State Opera, as it was called, was built in the late 1800s and it bore all the markings of that Renaissance Revival period.

When Jurgen knocked on their door that night, Hadley was ready. Her aunt sat in one of the wing chairs at the fireplace, looking ready for the evening in her shimmery red top and long skirt. The focal point of her outfit was a beautiful gold necklace with a knot design. Uncle Oscar had given her the piece long ago and Hadley knew it was filled with happy memories.

"Come in!" Hadley opened the door wider and Clara was the first person inside. "You look beautiful, Clara."

"Thank you." Suddenly Clara was shy. Her curls remained in place, probably from the spray they'd used in the spa that afternoon. Her green and red plaid taffeta dress was complemented by a warm black shrug. Although Clara looked darling, Hadley's attention was quickly caught by her father. Yes, Jurgen had looked handsome in his velvet jackets but this black tuxedo took him to a new level. Around his neck was a red cashmere scarf and a black coat hung over one arm. In his lapel was a red rose.

"I feel a bit underdressed." Stepping aside, Hadley ran one hand over her hip. The long black dress was her go-to outfit for fundraisers and client affairs. Floor length with a cowl neckline and dolman sleeves, the dress could be dressed up or down. Tonight she'd done everything to help the dress fit the occasion and Aunt Ethel had helped with an emerald necklace and earrings.

And then there were her heels. Usually Hadley's black heels made her taller than any of the men in the room. When she'd worn this dress with Brock, they were about the same height. But not tonight. Jurgen was at least two or three inches taller than Hadley.

But right now the man seemed speechless. Really? Was he at a loss for words? Maybe her imagination was playing tricks on her but his eyes did all the talking. Behind her, Clara was draped over the arm of Aunt Ethel's chair. "Doesn't Hadley look pretty?"

"Oh, I quite agree." But her aunt wasn't looking at Hadley. Her eyes were on Jurgen.

"Beyond pretty. Beyond beautiful," he finally said.

When Hadley turned back to him, Jurgen's eyes were pots of warm chocolate. Then his gaze shifted to her necklace. "That is a very special piece of jewelry."

Her fingers went to the stone. She was saving her Christmas present for New Year's Eve, but this emerald set was a close second. "Oh, this isn't mine. Aunt Ethel came to my rescue."

When she saw Hadley's dress laid out on the bed that evening, her aunt had hurried back to the safe in her room. Hadley had heard it open and close, followed by the metallic whirr of the lock.

One of the many things Hadley learned about her aunt during this trip was that she always traveled with her favorite jewelry in her travel case.

The emerald stone in the necklace was superb, complemented by the smaller stones in the drop earrings. Hadley had seen her aunt wear this set only a couple of times. And if she remembered correctly, both times she had been with Uncle Oscar. Wearing the emeralds made Hadley more than a little nervous, but her aunt had insisted.

Clearing his throat, Jurgen pulled his attention away. As she reached behind her for the red cape, Jurgen scooped it from the back of the sofa. "Won't you be warm with this in the opera house?"

"Yes, but will I be warm enough without it on the ride over?" She hesitated. Everything she felt in this moment was new and more than a little overwhelming. "Sometimes the bus can be chilly."

"I've made arrangements for a limousine for this evening."

"But of course," her aunt said, sounding pleased. "Then maybe just a shawl will do."

Clara spun around in her long green and black dress. The rustle of taffeta was in Hadley's ears as she went to get her Monet shawl. Months ago, the shawl had caught her eye as she hurried past the Michigan Avenue store. Maybe it was the seasonal display or the fact that she'd always loved Monet's work—she had to have it.

By the time she returned to the salon, her aunt stood there with her black fringed shawl swirled around her neck and that twinkle in her eye.

"May I?" Jurgen asked, already reaching for Hadley's shawl.

"Of course." Her legs felt weak.

"When will I get to wear a shawl?" Clara asked as they entered the elevator.

"When you stop racing through the halls," her father answered.

In the reception area downstairs, guests were going in for dinner. Hadley felt a little self-conscious when people turned to stare. Then she saw them. The men in black were also in the area, talking into their lapels.

"Who are those men?" She drew closer to her aunt but Jurgen overheard her question.

"Employees of the cruise line or so I would imagine. We should move along."

Outside, a limousine sat waiting. When the driver opened the door, Hadley stepped inside. The interior looked more like a cocktail lounge than a limo. Tufted seats extended to the back with tables in between. Miss Schmidt and Emerson gave them a quick wave from the back.

"Are we going to have refreshments again, Papa?" Clara asked.

"Not this time. The ride is short and you don't want to ruin that beautiful dress, do you?" Clara sighed dramatically and then again checked her curls.

"My goodness," Aunt Ethel said as they both took seats." I could really get used to this."

"Do you often travel in a limousine?" Hadley asked Jurgen teasingly. They were sitting across from each other at one of the tables. She wished that she had been able to figure out what he did for a living. The extravagance of the last few days had made her more curious.

"Yes," he said playfully. "But only when convenient."

Sitting next to Hadley, Clara patted her hand. "Don't you like sitting in the limousine, Hadley? It saves time. Miss Schmidt always tells me that. Do not keep the chauffeur waiting."

"Yes of course." Hadley tried not to laugh at Clara's imitation of Miss Schmidt.

"Vienna is even more enchanting at night. We can look at all the lights." With the touch of a button, Jurgen lowered the glass between the passengers and the driver. "Kurt, please go past the Belvedere Palace. I think the ladies would like to see it tonight."

"Yes, this is where we were yesterday," Aunt Ethel said.

Seeing the Belvedere Palace from the base of the hill gave Hadley the shivers. "How beautiful."

"Yes and very old." Jurgen studied the pattern of lights with appreciation. Every tree and bush on the property was lit up. And the building itself was strategically lit to illuminate the palace, which was a masterpiece.

Within minutes, they were back in the historical district. Shoppers and tourists filled the streets. Up ahead was the opera house. The warm yellow lighting on the cream-colored stone made the historical structure even more beautiful. Looking at her smiling aunt, she thought of all the exciting adventures Aunt Ethel had experienced during her lifetime. She may not have had children, but she certainly had gathered good memories.

Instead of stopping in the front where lines of people waited to be admitted, the limousine pulled around to the side into a private lane. In no time at all they were whisked through the door and into the caverness opera house. Glancing around at all of the marble and gold fixtures, Hadley was left speechless. The broad staircase, the generous banisters, the glittering chandeliers were all from a different era and gorgeously preserved.

"Have you ever been to the Paris opera house?" Jurgen asked.

Was he kidding? Hadley laughed. "No. I'll have to put that on my bucket list."

"You are too funny," her aunt said as they took a stairway to the side. "A bucket list. At your age."

"The Paris Opera House is very similar to this one…and well worth being on anyone's bucket list," he said with a grin.

Throngs of people moved up the central staircase marked by a green runner. But Jurgen had shown them to a smaller staircase to one side. If Emerson and Miss Schmidt had visited the opera house before, they gave no notice. They were all eyes as they went up the stairs. Then suddenly they were in the box which was absolutely mind blowing. "What does your friend do for a living?" Hadley asked.

"He enjoys life." And then Jurgen laughed as if he had made a funny joke. Sometimes she didn't know how to take him. "Ladies?" Jurgen motioned to the front row of four seats. Aunt Ethel entered the row as if she'd done this many times before. Holding her breath, Hadley followed. This night felt surreal, like one of those movies on late night TV. All the seats were angled toward the stage, unlike the block of seats below.

Down on the first floor almost all the seats were taken. The noise level rose and Hadley was able to forget the unpleasant emails with Brock. Should she feel responsible because he couldn't see Vienna? He'd tried to make her feel guilty about that. But not anymore.

The orchestra was tuning up. She could feel the strings and horns in her chest. Clara was sitting between Aunt Ethel and Hadley. At the last minute, Miss Schmidt scurried into the back row, followed by Emerson and Jurgen. She murmured that the height was making her nervous.

Down below, a low murmur of conversation bubbled. Every so often Jurgen would lean forward to point something out. In those moments Hadley could catch a whiff of his aftershave or feel the brief touch of his hand. Was she excited because she had never dreamed of seeing this ballet in Vienna? No, this feeling churning inside was more than that. In the past few days she'd come to know a man who was not only attractive and funny but a very good father.

Never had she dreamed that fatherhood could be so attractive on a man. Her brother Kevin was a great dad and spent a lot of time with his boys. More than once she'd seen him playing soccer in the side yard or heard about him taking them on a Saturday grocery store run to give Mindy a break.

But Jurgen's situation was different. He had experienced great sadness and yet he'd risen above that loss to parent Clara. And he'd done a great job. Although she would never see it, Hadley bet that he would create a skating rink for his daughter when they reached home—wherever that might be. Picturing Jurgen out in the backyard with the hose and sub-freezing weather was a stretch.

Emerson had handed out programs and she pored over the pictures with Clara. Then it was time. The dark claret curtains were swept aside and the production began. Clara could hardly contain herself. There were moments when Hadley reached out to pull the little girl back from the edge of the box. She was afraid that in her excitement Clara might lose her balance, although falling would be difficult to do. Safety precautions had been taken.

They all became swept up by the color and the movement on the stage below. The dance that was most entrancing for Clara was the one that involved a little girl with her name and the nutcracker. "Hadley, her name is Clara!"

Hadley only nodded and smiled while Aunt Ethel whipped out her opera glasses and then handed them to Clara. The Christmas tree on the set was spectacular and the dance of the parents made her smile. But when the nutcracker battled the mole, Clara drew back. Hadley squeezed her hand to reassure her.

"This is just a play," Jurgen leaned over to whisper to his daughter. "Pretend you are watching it on TV." Hadley heard the concern in his voice and saw Clara relax. The little girl looked so cute lifting the opera glasses. The first act passed all too quickly.

Before she knew it, the lights went up and people stood. "Intermission." Jurgen got to his feet. "Would anyone like anything?"

"A little champagne would be wonderful," Aunt Ethel piped

up.

"Emerson?" Jurgen turned to his valet and Hadley smiled. Emerson was Jurgen's Miranda. Now that she thought of it, she hadn't heard from her assistant for a while. She'd have to catch up with her soon.

When they left the box and filed out into the hallway, she noticed the men in dark suits. "Have they followed us here from the ship? They look so sinister."

Jurgen casually turned to study them. "They're just people who make sure things happen safely."

The comment made her a little nervous. "Are we in any danger here?"

"No, please relax." Turning, Jurgen hugged her. The movement came so naturally and caught her by surprise. Her breath felt tight in her throat. Did he feel something too? Giving a little laugh, he dropped his arm and looked away. Yes, maybe he did.

Just then, Aunt Ethel turned. Seeing them together, she sent Hadley a pleased smile and pulled her shawl tighter. "How lovely to be seated in this upper loggia," she told Jurgen. "But I think we'll leave you for just a second. Come, Clara." Before Hadley could even ask a question, her aunt, Miss Schmidt and Clara had disappeared, probably headed to the ladies room.

Then they were alone. Behind one of the claret curtains, they seemed to have total privacy.

"You look very beautiful tonight. I like your hair that way." The comment was casual and yet personal. His eyes roamed over her hair and Hadley patted the style that was unusual for her. The updo was more formal and wouldn't last long in Chicago's bitter wind.

"Courtesy of the hairstylist today," she said with a nervous laugh. "My hairdo was chosen to do justice to my aunt's emerald earrings."

"Very regal. You wear jewelry well."

"You look pretty good yourself tonight. Very handsome." What was she saying? The words were spilling out, unchecked. But truthfully, she'd never seen a tux look so good on a man.

"Are you looking forward to going home?"

"Not really. Actually, I feel a little sad." Why was she being so honest with him?

"Really?" Jurgen seemed to take that in. "I suppose you'll miss Shatzi."

Shaking her head slowly, she wondered why she felt this way. "I think it's more than Shatzi. Your little girl has stolen my heart."

"I think Clara feels strongly about you as well." Jurgen was doing that thing again where he cupped her elbow in his palm. They were so close that she could see a green ring around his dark iris. See the pulse throbbing in his throat.

"Is it warm in here or is it me?" Hadley began to fan herself with a program.

His eyes twinkled. "Not really. What would give you that becoming blush in your cheeks?"

She stopped fanning. "Are you flirting with me?"

"Would that bother you?"

"I don't think so. But it is surprising."

"It shouldn't be." He traced her jawline with a finger. "I'm going to miss you, Hadley Parker. Very, very much." His words closed on a husky whisper. "And I'm asking myself why."

She had to lean closer to hear the last words. In her head she was doing a happy dance. But she couldn't let him know. Hadley wanted to sort out all the feelings overtaking her. "When you figure that out, let me know, okay?"

His kiss took those last words from her lips. Jurgen's kiss was warm and soothing and right, and so was the hand around her waist. One palm on his chest, she pushed back and caught the surprise in his eyes.

"I'm thinking that…" he began.

Suddenly, a camera flashed. At least, Hadley thought it was a camera. But when she turned, all she saw were the two security guards. Not again. Those guys were creepy. "Those men again."

Following her eyes, Jurgen turned and snapped his fingers. Just like that, they melted back into the corridor. *Really?* Maybe people did that in Vienna. Just snapped their fingers at potential muggers and they disappeared.

Okay, that sounded weird. But at that moment weird things were dancing through her head. Hadley breathed him in, noticing every little thing. She wanted to trace the faint scar above his left eye with a finger. Leaning against the wall, Jurgen looked so very sad.

"Back to missing you, Hadley. What are your plans now that you no longer wear an engagement ring?" Taking her left hand, he ran his fingers lightly down her ring finger. She thought she might faint.

"I don't really have any plans." Was she sad or relieved? Hadley felt overwhelmed when she thought of everything she had to do when she got home. All of those wedding cancellations. But Miranda could help. "I nearly made a terrible mistake."

"But you changed direction?"

"Yes, I've changed direction." She gave a little laugh. "But now I don't know where I'm going."

"You really don't know?"

Was he going to kiss her again? Her head pounded and she felt so warm. Maybe she shouldn't have worn this long, knit dress, although Jurgen seemed to like it.

"Your Royal Highness? Jurgen, is that you?"

Royal what? Jerking away, Hadley looked over at an older couple and an attractive dark-haired woman standing a few feet away. She waited for Jurgen to tell them they were mistaken.

Irritation ruffling his brow, Jurgen gave a little bow. "Marceline, how nice to see you and Edgar. We are taking a little holiday break, Clara and I."

"You remember our daughter, Francine."

"Yes, yes of course." Jurgen threw Hadley a nervous look.

Both women dipped into a curtsy, while at the same time Aunt Ethel appeared. Clara had something in her hand. "Well, what do you have there?" Hadley asked, grateful for the interruption.

"A little memento," her aunt said, throwing a curious look at the newcomers. "Something to remember us by."

"I'm going to name her Mia," Clara said in an excited voice as she held out the exquisite little ballerina doll.

"Always visit the gift shop in places like this," Aunt Ethel commented." You find the nicest things. But we seem to have lost Miss Schmidt along the way."

Hadley hardly registered the conversation. She was almost relieved when her aunt pulled her back into their balcony. Jurgen had somehow dispatched the older couple. "I'd like to explain," he whispered in her ear as she sat down.

Your Royal Highness? Really?

Down below, she watched the couple and their daughter take their seats in the center section. Obviously excited, they spoke to the people in the next row. Together, their faces lifted to the box and they sure weren't looking at Hadley. To her amazement, Clara noticed them with a nod and lifted her hand. The only time she'd seen that royal wave was on TV when the Windsors greeted their people from the royal balcony. Clara did it so naturally.

The lights blinked and the theater darkened. Hadley felt grateful for the darkness. Clara had gotten up and she talked to Miss Schmidt, who had returned. Together they left, probably to go back to the restroom. They were only gone a short while.

While Clara and the others were swept up into the dances, Hadley was still processing what had happened. Every time Jurgen moved in the chair behind her, she remembered the kiss. That kiss.

And Jurgen. But who was he?

Chapter 21

Why hadn't he told her the truth? Hadley felt Aunt Ethel's eyes on her. What did her aunt know about Jurgen? Was that why she was reading that book on European royalty on the activity deck that day?

That evening she had basked in Jurgen's smile. But who was he, really? As the ballerinas performed the Mandarin tea dances on the stage below, Hadley felt sick. Thank goodness Clara was spellbound. The little girl didn't know how confused Hadley was right now. All those comments. The castles, the horses, the references she never understood.

But somehow her aunt knew. Hadley couldn't even look over at her. And behind her, she heard Jurgen breathing, as if he were leaning closer. But maybe she was just imagining things. Once or twice she thought she felt the touch of his hand on her shoulder. But she was probably imagining that too.

This cruise had been an escape but in the wonderful, warm feeling of the season had she completely lost her head? And possibly, her heart?

When Mother Ginger came out with her voluminous skirt that hid all her children until they scattered and danced, Hadley laughed with the rest of the audience. But the laugh had a sharp edge. For a second, she was tempted to leave and walk out onto the concourse to calm herself. But Jurgen might follow her. And then where would she be? What was he hiding?

But the kind, gentle father she'd witnessed during this trip was real. That much she knew. One glance at the little girl next to her told Hadley she could never think that of Clara's "papa." Mesmerized by the scene below, Clara sat at the edge of her chair.

Would this ballet never end? Hadley wanted so desperately to leave. Finally came the wonderful dance of the flowers. Her heart lifted, even though she had no reason for that. She could feel Aunt Ethel giving her quizzical glances while panic raged through her.

When Jurgen tried to speak to her in an undertone, Hadley couldn't answer. Couldn't turn. She was a terrible judge of men. Although Hadley had always thought of herself as a sophisticated businesswoman who knew who she was and what she wanted, she was really naïve. And she was certainly no match for this cosmopolitan group, especially Jurgen.

As the sugarplum fairy made her entrance and danced with the handsome cavalier, Hadley's heart broke. This is just a performance, she told herself. Just a play. Eyes sparkling, Clara sat there entranced. Who could blame her? Below them was the fairy tale, but Hadley wanted this in real life. And she kept getting it wrong.

Oh, why hadn't she tucked a tissue in her little clutch? When Clara mumbled something about her doll, Hadley hardly heard her. The ballet ended and the applause was thunderous and continued while the talented cast was called out again and again into the bright lights.

And then it was over. The audience began to leave. Jurgen's security patrol appeared to escort them down the stairway and into the limousine. Finally she understood their role and why they were lurking about. They were protecting Jurgen and his daughter. Down below the crowds were streaming from the main floor. Getting up, Hadley looked around. Her heart froze. No Clara. Had she already gone out into the hall? Hadley turned.

"Where is Clara?" Jurgen's face paled.

From the way Miss Schmidt was rubbing her eyes, Hadley suspected she may have fallen asleep. "I think she said something about her doll," Hadley mumbled. Why couldn't she remember?

Jurgen turned. "What exactly did she say?"

Hadley felt her eyes fill. "I don't know. Something about the doll."

"I will go and see immediately." Miss Schmidt stumbled from the box.

"And I'll check with security." Emerson shot out into the hallway.

Meanwhile Aunt Ethel had lifted her opera glasses and was scanning the crowd below. Then she turned the glasses on the boxes across from them and around the loggia. Turning, she squeezed Hadley's hand. "I'm sure they'll find her, dear."

"But there are so many people and she's so small." Hadley's head spun as she looked down. And they were royalty. Clara was a princess. Articles about kidnappings for ransom seemed to fill the papers every day.

Clara had been sitting right next to her. Why hadn't she paid more attention? When Emerson burst out of the stairwell, the two men in black followed. "They were taking a break," he muttered to Jurgen.

"What? A smoking break?" Jurgen turned pale. "My men? I can't believe it." He took a phone from his inner pocket—one she had never seen him use. She had to find Clara.

When the lights flashed, everyone froze. "Would you please return to your seats," a voice said over the sound system. Down below and in the boxes all around them, people looked at each other. What was happening? No one seemed to know. "Everyone, return to your seats immediately." The voice came again and this time it was a command.

But no way was Hadley returning to her seat. "I have to search for her," she told Aunt Ethel.

"Of course. Yes, go." Aunt Ethel sat down in the nearest chair as if this was all too much for her.

Turning, she faced Miss Schmidt, who looked as if she might faint at any moment. "What exactly did Clara say when she left?" *And why weren't you with her?*

"The doll. Something about the d-doll." But the older woman was having trouble getting her words out. "She was looking for it."

"Where would she have left it?"

"Probably in the restroom. Or behind the curtain. She kept playing behind some of these curtains." And she flipped one of the heavy draperies with her fingers. What was Miss Schmidt doing while all that was going on? *And what was I doing?*

Hadley flew out of the box, brushing past Jurgen as she left. Talking to one of the security guards, he barely noticed she was leaving. Following the discreet signs, she dashed down the hallway and into the women's restroom closest to where they'd been sitting. "Clara! Clara!"

A woman was standing at one of the sinks, talking on her phone. "Little girl," Hadley threw at her. "Looking for her doll?"

But the woman shook her head and went back to her conversation, dabbing gloss on her lips as she talked. Outside in the hallway, Hadley zigzagged through the people who were slowly returning to their seats. The ushers were moving through the crowd, politely encouraging everyone to "please take your seats." No one seemed to be in any hurry. They didn't understand. Hadley wanted to scream.

The other restrooms on that floor were also empty. Hadley's voice echoed against the marble as she called Clara's name. Why hadn't she paid more attention? She'd sat in her seat thinking about Jurgen. Foolish thoughts, while Clara disappeared. Reaching one of the side stairways, she started to climb, taking the stairs two at a time. If she ripped the back slit in this dress, she didn't care.

Her breath came in short hard gasps that tore at her chest as she ran from restroom to restroom on the third floor, calling Clara's name. This might be useless. If Clara had left the doll in a restroom, it was probably the one nearest their box. But then again, Clara was seven and curious. She was used to exploring everywhere safely. Where had Jurgen's security men been while Clara wandered away? Smoking? Anger pulsed in Hadley's head. She wanted to wring their necks.

While she checked all the restrooms on the floor above where they have been sitting, Hadley ran into a woman who looked official. "I'm working upward," she told the uniformed woman, who nodded. "If you could check the restrooms at ground level, then we would have it covered. Her name is Clara." With a quick nod of her head, the woman took off and Hadley slammed through the door of the next restroom. Nothing.

This was what it was like to be a parent. The thought hit her while she sprinted up the steps to the floor above. Children made you vulnerable. Was this why Brock didn't want to have kids? Was he wiser than she was?

The hallway was quiet. What floor was she on now? This area must have emptied before the announcement was made. Hadley battled hopelessness. Why would that little girl ever have climbed this high?

"Clara! Clara!" She poked her head into another women's restroom.

"What?" That tiny, slightly annoyed voice was unmistakable.

Hadley burst through the inner door. There Clara stood in her taffeta Christmas dress. Standing on her tippy toes at one of the sinks, she was squirting hand cream into her tiny palm. Propped against the mirror, her new doll stood watching. "I'm teaching Mia how to take care of her manicure." Clara spread out her fingers and wiggled them. The tiny trees on her shiny red nails caught the light.

"We've been looking all over for you, sweetheart." Stooping,

Hadley opened her arms. Never had anything felt as good as Clara's slim figure wrapped in Hadley's arms. "I was so worried."

Frowning, Clara pulled back. "Are you crying?" She touched a hand to Hadley's damp cheek.

"Yes, you little stinker. I'm crying. We didn't know where you were. What are you doing up here?"

"I told you, teaching Mia about her manicure." And she sniffed as if to say, *how dare you ask that question*. "Mia was lost."

Hadley let that sink in. "So, did you lose her up here?"

Clara smoothed a hand over the ballerina's golden hair. "Oh no. I found her downstairs. But we needed our privacy."

Hadley had no idea what kind of rules this child followed. Maybe none. "Come on, then. Your father is very concerned." Crazed with worry would be more like it. After Clara had tucked Mia under one arm, she took Hadley's hand and they left. The stillness of the upper floor surrounded them with an eerie silence. Anything could have happened up here. But it didn't. Hadley had to squelch her imagination or she'd start sobbing again.

When they reached their box seats, Jurgen was talking to some of the security men. His face was pale and taut. Although he was probably scared to death, he was still very much in charge. But when he saw them coming through the clusters of people still in the hallway, he hurried toward them. "Clara, where have you been?"

By this time, Clara knew how serious the situation was. Her father swept her up into his arms. Patting his cheek, she said, "Papa, you don't have to worry about me." *Seven going on seventy*.

That was Clara.

"Did you find her?" Aunt Ethel asked as Hadley stumbled out onto the balcony and collapsed in the nearest chair.

"Yes." And she quickly related the story.

"So I guess we won't be having another spa day soon."

"Easy for you to joke. I was scared to death."

"Of course you were." Her aunt hugged her. "We all love that little girl. But oh my, she is her own person."

"I fully realize that now. Especially after hearing that Jurgen is, well, royalty."

An announcement came over the sound system and a sigh of relief ran through the theater. No explanation was given for the delay. Everyone could now leave. Spilling from the doorways, people just wanted to get home or onto their next destination.

Without another word, Jurgen led them down the steps to where the limousine was waiting. The drive back to the ship was silent. For a while, Clara talked animatedly with her doll. Catching Hadley's eye, Aunt Ethel raised her brows as if to say, *why did I ever buy that for her?*

The lights of Vienna were still beautiful but Hadley felt empty. Maybe the near loss had done that. Reaching up, she felt her right ear, mainly because it didn't pinch like the left one. *Perfect.* Somehow she'd lost her right emerald earring, maybe because it was a clip-on, which she rarely wore. Sitting there in the dark, her Monet shawl around her, she decided to wait until tomorrow to tell her aunt. When she got back to her room, her mind was still racing. Opening her laptop, she sent an email off to Miranda with twelve points. Nothing else was working in her life, but she could at least organize her business before her return.

Chapter 22

The note slipped under her door simply said, "Thought you could use some rest. Going to breakfast, if you need me. Love, AE." After last night, Hadley felt relieved to be alone. She wanted to process things. Still wearing sleep pants and a T-shirt, she stumbled into the salon. Like an accident victim, she didn't know where she was or what had happened.

Her aunt must have opened the drapes. Budapest lay before her, its buildings reflected in the river. Over the past ten days or so, she'd seen enough buildings to last her for a while. The beautiful stone structures from centuries gone by were all melting into each other. Hadley was in a bad mood.

And she needed coffee. Her stomach was rumbling and she checked her phone. It had been a long time since she'd slept until ten o'clock. And had she really slept? Last night had been restless for her and filled with nightmares. In her dream she was lost in a fog, much like the fogs that sometimes shrouded the ship. Running through a big leafy area that felt like a park, she was looking for something. But she couldn't find it. The sense of loss engulfed her.

Trying to shake off that terrible mood, she took a long shower, flipping the levers back-and-forth from hot to cold. But she didn't have time to dry her hair. So after she stepped from the shower and into one of the plush robes, she pulled her hair back into one French braid. At least they'd found Clara. That was the one good thing that had come out of last night. Poor Jurgen had been wild with worry.

Jurgen. But she just couldn't go there.

As she entered the dining room a short time later, she ran into Aunt Ethel who seemed to be on her way out. Emerson was with her.

"We thought we'd go up topside," her aunt told her calmly, as if she hung out with Emerson every day. "See more of Budapest from up there."

"Great idea."

"Feel free to join us." Her aunt was dressed in a blue track suit. She must have bought the matching pants and jacket for one of the exercise classes she occasionally took at her club. Although Aunt Ethel didn't work out very much—a walk around the block tired her—she liked to look the part. Her tennis shoes were also blue, accented with silver piping. Hadley smiled at the studs twinkling on the toes. This was definitely a dress-down day. Even Emerson seemed much more casual today. A brown plaid shirt topped with a quilted vest had replaced his standard suit and tie.

"See you later." She kissed her aunt's cheek. "Think I'll just grab some coffee and a schnecken."

"All right, dear. I took the liberty of signing us up for a tour of Budapest this afternoon. But if you're not up for it…"

"Let me think about that." From the corner of her eye, she

spotted Clara and Jurgen at a table near the window. No way could she handle them this morning. As soon as her aunt and Emerson had disappeared up the stairway, Hadley took off for the back of the ship. The more casual restaurant back there was serving coffee and yes, they still had one of the buttery schneckens.

The back of the restaurant was left open by sliding glass windows. Hadley took a seat at one of the tables that overlooked the water. Living near Lake Michigan, she was used to the water. But this was the Danube and she was in their final days.

The trip was ending. A sadness came over her and she wished she could shake it off. Last night had seemed so beautiful at first. And then it had become unexpectedly exciting. During those few private moments with Jurgen, she felt something was about to happen. But she didn't know what. All that had ended when Clara went missing.

Losing Clara had frightened her in many ways. Not only was she worried about the little girl, she also wondered about herself as she searched for Clara. How could she care so deeply about this child she had not known existed two weeks ago? Sipping her peppermint coffee took her back to the excursions they'd shared. When she returned to Chicago, she would take those wonderful memories with her. Hadley sure wished she felt better about that.

Pinching a corner of her schnecken, she unwound it. For the last few days, she hadn't thought about counting calories. Maybe her jeans were a little snug. Who cared? When she got back, she would have time to diet. She'd return to that crazy pace that she now hated. In the mornings, she'd get up at five so that she could hit the fitness club before starting her schedule. These luxurious mornings in bed would come back to her.

Relaxation. Enjoying culture and art. How could she make them part of her life? But a hole would still be there. And only two people could fill that void.

Taking her phone from her pocket, Hadley opened her emails. Miranda had sent her a list of questions and she sighed. This would be easier if she called her assistant. She could do that later. Discussing proposals, meetings and open houses would occupy her mind. But she was so tired of it all.

Before she knew it, the pastry was gone. But the buttery taste lingered on her tongue. Why hurry back to the room? Lights glowed along the Danube and holiday decorations reflected in the water. She signaled for another mug of coffee. Sitting in the sunlight felt so pleasant. Maybe she would take that tour with her aunt that afternoon. Would Emerson be going along? She smiled.

***

"Why didn't Hadley want to sit with us?" Clara asked. Jurgen hated the tears in her voice. Hadn't they had enough tears in the past? "Is she mad at me? Is she mad that I got lost last night?"

"She probably didn't see us sitting here." Jurgen studied the archway where Hadley had stood, talking to her aunt. Maybe she'd return. There were so many things he wanted to talk to her about.

"But I was waving at her!" Clara was getting cross. Last night she'd been up way past her bedtime. "I think she saw me."

Jurgen hoped that wasn't true. Because if she was ignoring Clara then she was ignoring him too. "Just because you want something to be true doesn't mean it is." Okay that was a little confusing. Even he couldn't follow the direction of his words. Dancing her ballerina across the table top, Clara said, "But I want to talk to her this morning. Mia does too."

Great. Now he not only had to deal with his daughter. He also had to deal with her doll. "I'm sure she'll be around later. Maybe she'll be on the bus trip."

"I don't want to go on the bus trip unless Hadley is going too." Her lower lip trembled. Maybe building this friendship with Hadley had been a bad idea.

"But if you don't go on the bus trip, what will you do?" He couldn't leave Clara here with Miss Schmidt. The lack of responsibility she'd shown at the opera house was inexcusable. When they returned to Starengard, he would have to make some decisions. Jurgen would consult with his legal team about the process of retiring a staff member. And he didn't intend to include his mother in that consultation.

"I could stay here and play with Shatzi."

That was another sore point. "I think Shatzi will be glad to be home. She doesn't like being on the ship. It's only natural. She misses being outside. In fact, maybe we could take her for a walk this morning. The trip is almost over and I no longer care if people see her." The truth was, he could use a walk too. He may have to rethink the rules about pets on the ships.

"Can I hold the leash?" Clara slipped off her chair. Dressed in navy blue corduroy slacks and a navy and red top, she looked cute.

His mother would agree that her wardrobe had improved. Hadley had been a big influence on his daughter. But those red cowboy boots on her feet might not pass with the queen, not that her approval mattered much anymore.

Over the past two weeks he'd had a lot of hands-on time with Clara. Time that he treasured. But he still hadn't gotten the hang of those braids. He probably never would. Today her hair was in pigtails. But when Clara turned around to search the doorway again, Jurgen could see that the part in the back was crooked.

So be it. Those red fingernails with little green trees made him smile every time he caught her looking at them. That was the result of what he thought of as the Hadley Influence. And he thoroughly approved.

Fifteen minutes later, they were walking down the gangplank, bundled up in their winter coats. Clara wore her green hat and scarf over her red coat. A cardinal flitted past and Shatzi took off. Thank goodness Jurgen still had the leash. Shatzi was barking like crazy so Jurgen held on tight until the bird had flown away. For a while they followed a path along the water, enjoying the morning air. Little Shatzi was loving it, marching along, head up and tail wagging furiously. The dog probably got her attitude from Clara.

"Papa?" his little girl began. What now? He recognized the wheedling tone of her voice and hoped that he had the answer.

"I'm going to miss Hadley."

Jurgen almost laughed. Clara said this as if Hadley was a school friend she hung out with when they went skiing in Switzerland, not an adult woman she'd befriended on this trip. "Are you going to miss her too?"

"Oh yes. I most certainly will." He'd gotten up early that morning and quickly dressed in his workout clothes. Clara was still fast asleep and if he had awakened Miss Schmidt with his call, that was too bad. Sleepy-eyed, she'd arrived to stay with Clara and he'd taken off. When Hadley wasn't on the running track, he moved down to the fitness center. But she wasn't there either. His frustration built. He'd wanted to talk to her about last night. Was she avoiding him?

Maybe she was just tired. And maybe she was tired of him and Clara.

Emerson had retrieved the security tapes from the opera house. After Clara had fallen asleep, Jurgen had watched the tapes again and again, hopping from floor to floor. The sheer terror on Hadley's face and her tears told him so much. She felt deeply for his daughter. Her tears moved him.

But how did she feel about Clara's father?

Chapter 23

Back in the suite, Hadley decided to call Miranda. They could catch up and make sure things happened as planned upon Hadley's return. She had her assistant's list right in front of her.

The two of them had been together for about three years. Lately Miranda seemed absent minded, but that was nothing new. Hadley wondered if she was seeing someone new again. Her assistant went through men like potato chips. The phone rang and rang. What time was it in Chicago? Hadley thumbed through her phone. Okay, kind of early but usually Miranda was up. Hadley was ready to leave a message when the phone picked up. "Hey, it's Hadley. Am I calling too early?" This was New Year's Eve but usually they worked on this day until about two.

"I'm up." Miranda gave what sounded like a big yawn. "Sick as a dog all night."

"Sorry to hear that. Too many margaritas and a late night out?"

"Not really. Think I got a bad burger."

"I thought you didn't eat burgers." Miranda had been a confirmed vegan for a long time. She was always passing out healthy eating tips.

"Right. Something new. But not for long."

"Okay, got a pen?" Grabbing her list, Hadley took her through the first two or three items. "If you write rough drafts for those proposals, I can go through them more quickly when I get home."

"Got it. So, are you having a good time over there?"

"Yes, and so is my aunt. It's been nice hanging out together." Silence. Hadley was still thinking about that burger. That was so unlike Miranda.

"Who's the hunk in your Facebook posts?"

Hadley tore her attention back to the call. "I didn't know you did much with Facebook. Thought you were more Instagram."

"Yeah, well, one of my friends told me about you ice-skating with some awesome, hot guy and a little girl."

"Really?" Suddenly something hit her like a punch in the gut. How could she have been so foolish? "Have you seen Brock lately?"

"No. Not really."

Hadley wasn't convinced. "Well then, have you seen my sister-in-law?" Mindy had known Miranda from high school, and Mindy used Facebook.

"Absolutely not. Are you kidding? All she does is talk about kids. Boring."

Pieces of the puzzle began to fit together. But Hadley wanted to wait until she got home to deal with it. She was just about to wrap up the call when she thought she heard a door open and close on Miranda's end. Her bedroom was near the front door. "Delivery boy! Coffee and bagels!"

Miranda muffled the phone. "One minute." But it was too late.

How many times had Brock called that out when he returned from an early morning bagel run? Too many. Now Hadley really felt sick. And angry.

"Say hi to Brock," Hadley said and she hung up.

Wow. The desk chair creaked as she sat back. She'd really missed that one. Miranda had often acted as a go-between with Brock. If he was trying to reach Hadley with no luck, he would go through Miranda. When she was with a client, Hadley wouldn't answer her phone and it made him crazy.

Stunned, she walked out into the salon just as her aunt spun through the door, humming something that sounded like "We Wish You a Merry Christmas."

"You're a happy camper this morning." At least one of them felt good.

"Beautiful day up on that deck." Aunt Ethel dropped her keycard on the desk. "Did you have your breakfast?"

"Yes. Schneckens." So far, that had been the best part of her morning.

"Oh, yum." Glowing, Aunt Ethel sat down on the sofa and Hadley joined her.

Although she'd been dreading this, she had to tell her aunt about the emerald earring. "Aunt Ethel, I'm afraid I lost one of your earrings last night. I'm so sorry."

"Oh, dear. All that rushing around, trying to find Clara. But you found her, sweetheart. That's the important thing."

Only her aunt would have such a generous response—always thinking of someone else. "Yes, but those earrings. Uncle Oscar gave them to you." The tears came and Hadley couldn't stop them. And as she sobbed, she wondered. Was she crying about the earrings or her whole situation? Betrayed by a fiancé and mistaken about a man she admired very much. Well, more than admired. "Those earrings are one of your prize possessions. Somehow I'll make it up to you." But the earrings were a matched set so she didn't know how she could do that.

"Oh piffle." Aunt Ethel gave Hadley a hug. "It's just a piece of jewelry, Hadley. Certainly not worth your tears. Now, let me see."

Sitting on the sofa, she could see her aunt's mind working. "I think I'll just give Emerson a call," she finally said with a smile, as if she were looking forward to that call. Turning at the doorway, her aunt looked back at her. Wiping her tears away, Hadley must have looked like a mess. Where was the box of tissues?

"Life is about people, not things…don't you think?" her aunt asked gently. "During our remaining time of the ship, maybe you'd feel better concentrating on the people you've met. Things can be replaced. People? Not so much."

With that, her aunt disappeared into her room. How had Hadley missed this relationship developing between Aunt Ethel and Jurgen's assistant? But then again, she'd totally missed Brock and Miranda. All that pre-Christmas rushing around had absorbed all her attention.

That relationship between Brock and Miranda probably wouldn't last. Miranda wasn't known for lasting relationships. And she'd always made it known that children were not in her future. Some of that may have rubbed off on Brock. In any case, two doors were closing and she'd deal with that later.

What about the doors facing her now? What could she say or do?

Her aunt returned to the room. "Everything okay?" Hadley asked.

"Emerson's going to check with some contacts in Vienna. You know, at the opera house."

"You're too much. You do know that, right?" And Hadley couldn't leave it there. "What's going on between you two?"

Her aunt shifted a shoulder as she sat back down. "Emerson will be retiring soon. So we talked about that a little bit. Guess we're both at that age."

"Talked about what, if I could ask?"

"Oh, you know. Acclimating oneself to retirement." Her aunt was purposely being vague. She was really good at that.

"But I thought you'd never worked." Aunt Ethel had been in retirement ever since Hadley could remember.

Her dear aunt scrunched her lips to one side. She'd probably hate it if she knew what that did to those lines around her lips. "Sort of. I mean it wasn't my full-time job, but sometimes I would handle Oscar's books. That wasn't his forte. So have you changed your mind about the excursion this afternoon?"

"As a matter fact, I have." If Hadley stayed here on the ship, she'd do nothing but think about Brock and Miranda. And she didn't want to go there. The trip was almost over and when would she get to see Budapest again? And what about Jurgen and Clara? She hoped they'd be on the trip.

A knock came on the door, and her aunt went to answer it. "Oh look, Hadley. Roses."

***

Jurgen didn't want to take this call. But maybe he should face his mother now. There were so many things he had to clear up with her. "Mother. You're calling early."

"But not early enough. Have you seen today's copy of *The Sun*?"

"I thought we agreed that you would stop reading that trashy tabloid. It's disgusting. Every time anyone has the hint of a tip, they blow it into a malicious story. You know that. What is it this time?"

"You're only saying that because you're on the front cover. Who is that woman?"

His heart froze. Jurgen walked over to the laptop on his desk. "I don't know what you're talking about so you'll have to tell me." Speaking slowly to give himself time, he tapped *The Sun* into the browser bar. The picture that came up caught his breath. Hadley looked so beautiful as he kissed her at the opera. Hmm. They made an attractive couple. But who had taken this picture?

"Remember, Jurgen. You are the crown prince and will be king one day. You cannot go away on a two-week cruise and indulge in some dalliance with an American."

Oh, didn't he just wish? He had to read the story. "Mother, you're breaking up. And I have a… meeting soon. Talk to you later." With that he hung up. Hitting Print, he waited for the whirring sound from one of the cabinets. Then he retrieved the black and white copy, quickly scanned it and folded it into the pocket of his jacket.

***

Two hours later Jurgen was standing on one of the terraces in front of Buda Castle on the south side of the Danube. This castle and the area around it were rich with history. The cruise ships often brought people up here. About forty guests from the ship had encircled their guide. Jurgen wished the breeze would slacken. It was always so windy at this high point of the hill. Studying the Baroque style of the current castle, he couldn't imagine traipsing through these two hundred rooms every day. The security problems would be enormous, to say nothing of the upkeep.

But enough of the castle. Right now he was facing Hadley over the heads of the group. How could he get her alone? When he'd boarded the bus with Clara, the back seats were already filled. Hadley and her aunt were seated in the very final row. Jurgen had hoped that he would have time to talk to Hadley privately. Although he'd had a bouquet of roses sent that morning, he had no idea if they'd arrived.

Time was getting short. Tomorrow was New Year's Eve Day and the following day most of the guests would leave for their flights home.

As the guide blathered on about the rooms in this huge castle, he slowly moved over behind Hadley. Although her aunt saw him coming and gave him a smile, Hadley seemed to be in another world. Maybe she was already home, reuniting with her fiancé. Taking up her life and getting on with it. The thought gutted him.

When the guide continued describing the many rooms of the castle, he held everyone's attention. Well, except for Jurgen and Clara, who followed behind him. "Papa."

She pulled at his coat and he caught her hand. "Shh. Listen to the man."

Hadley was wearing the red hat they'd bought for her. The enormous silver pom-pom had flopped over into her eyes. Coming up behind her, he gently positioned the hat back on the center of her head. She jerked. Just as Hadley turned to look up at him, her Aunt Ethel bent down to whisper something to Clara. He didn't know what he'd do without her aunt.

Edging a fuming Hadley away from the group and under a portico, Jurgen felt at a loss for words. Those dark eyes wouldn't look up at him. "You've been avoiding me."

When she lifted her eyes, they were so troubled that something twisted inside him. Then she sighed. "You lied to me," she whispered. The group had moved away a bit and Aunt Ethel and Clara edged away with it.

"Forgive me, but I did not want you to know me as Your Royal Highness." His voice sounded tired, even to his own ears. "You're fun. Sweet and lively. Hadley, I wanted that life for just a few days. Is that so wrong?"

Did she just snort? "When were you going to tell me you were someone else? Someone with a crown on his head?" Color flushed her cheeks. Her delectable lips opened and closed. But he could not let himself drift off course.

"I'm sorry, but I didn't know what would happen. I never

expected to meet someone like you. I was, how do you say in America, blindsided?"

"You were?" she offered with a cute little shake of her head that indicated he was impossible. But he already knew that.

"Yes, blindsided." The air softened around them. The group had moved away and Aunt Ethel gave him signs with her hand. Jurgen nodded. Clara was safe with Hadley's aunt. He would catch up to them later. Ernst and Hans had been dismissed that morning. Emerson would screen candidates for their replacements. Back to his explanation. "I came on this cruise with my daughter to give her a happy Christmas. And then you…you took over. Everything changed."

Hadley's elegant brows came together in a frown. "What does that mean? I didn't take over anything."

Rarely was he called upon to explain things. In his world, people nodded in agreement with him. Not this woman. And he loved that about her. "Sometimes you challenge what I say or do. I find that refreshing."

"Let's go back to being blind-sided." Tilting her head, Hadley looked up at him, much the way Clara regarded him when she was considering what to say next. "Is that a bad thing or good thing? The challenging part, I mean."

"It depends. From your point of view, I suppose it's frustrating. For example, if you set the treadmill at an angle, you don't like someone pointing out that it could be dangerous. At that point, I should keep quiet."

"Oh, so we're back to the treadmill again." A tiny grin teased her lips. "Yes, you're right. You tend to judge things from your perspective."

"The treadmill is a symbol. A figure of speech."

"A simile? A metaphor?" Well, at least she was trying.

He had no clue. "Something like that. Instead of walking on the flat treadmill, you insist on raising it. In addition to that angle being dangerous, it makes your workout more difficult than it needs to be. Especially when you close your eyes so you can listen to Christmas music."

"Are you saying that I make life difficult for myself?"

"Maybe." He could be in dangerous territory here. "May I continue?"

She grimaced. "Yes. But it's funny you should say that. Other people have pointed that out to me."

"Excellent. Then maybe it's true. Sometimes." The breeze had loosened a strand of her soft hair. Jurgen reached for it. Yes, it felt as soft as it looked. Taking his time, he looped it behind her ear. "Maybe. Anyway, back to us."

"Is there an us?" She wrinkled her nose.

"Most certainly." Was he messing things up? "I came on this trip and had all kinds of plans for Clara. We would improve her manners. Maybe she would learn to eat more nutritious foods."

Crossing her arms, Hadley looked up at him. "Oh, right. That sounds like a lot of fun for a little girl."

"Yes, well. No doubt you're right." How could he ever have thought that Clara would enjoy this trip if he made it a teaching exercise? "Then you agreed to hide Shatzi."

"I had to," she sputtered, motioning to the Danube. "I thought you were going to throw that sweet little dog into the river."

"My daughter exaggerates and I understand why you thought that. But you are so wonderful, handling her."

"Thank you. I really like Clara." Her eyes darkened again.

"I know you do. And your presence has made our lives happier. Before I met you, my life was very… boring. I didn't know what to do about it. And I didn't want to try. Remember that day at the bridge? The bridge with all the locks?"

"Of course." And she sighed.

"Looking at all those locks, I realized that I had locked love *out* of my life. All those couples were locking love in."

She smiled. "An interesting observation."

"Now you are sounding like the royal therapist." They laughed together and it felt so good. "My little girl was a problem and my mother kept pointing that out every day."

"Clara is very special."

"I love the way you defend her." Coming closer, he fixed her hat again. Maybe they should've chosen a hat with a smaller pom-pom.

"You have to get rid of Miss Schmidt." Hadley spoke with such passion. "Clara needs to have someone young and optimistic around her. Certainly there are qualified nannies to fill that position."

"What if I want her to learn proper English? What if I want her to learn American manners?"

Another snort from Hadley. "Don't go overboard. Sometimes

Americans can be very presumptuous. I've noticed that on this trip. But then again. Sometimes a crown prince can be presumptuous too." Slanting her head, she cast a coy glance up at him through her eyelashes.

He swallowed hard. "Oh really? Do you find me presumptuous?" By this time they were alone, leaning against the warm stonework. The sun had come out.

"Sometimes." He was glad they could take their time with this conversation. The staff now understood Jurgen's position. The bus was not going to leave without him.

"Well, what are you going to do about it?" There was that challenge again.

"Maybe this…" And he kissed her. He'd been wanting to do that ever since the ballet. He'd needed a reality check. And yes. She was sweet and warm, and yet she set his whole body on fire. He could kiss her like this forever. But just when he was considering that, he heard the stamping of little cowboy boots behind him. "Papa, are you kissing Hadley?"

"Maybe we should leave them alone," Aunt Ethel said softly as Jurgen turned to see Emerson right behind her.

"And maybe we should leave this bus trip." Stepping aside, he asked Emerson to have a limousine pick him up at the Waltzer Café on Castle Hill.

After a quick lunch at the café, the limousine took them to a place that he thought both Hadley and Clara would enjoy. The pinball museum, also called the flipper museum, was very popular with all ages.

"At this museum, we can all become children again." Of course Emerson and Aunt Ethel came with them. He was happy to see the two older people enjoying each other's company. They deserved each other. Emerson would be retiring soon and Jurgen would made arrangements to deed over a cottage on the estate.

This trip had given him a new perspective on his kingdom and how things must be. And since he saw the road ahead, he felt strongly that he would make it the way he wanted it.

As they played with a *Twilight* pinball machine, he enjoyed Hadley's laugh and her smile. Clara's too. She had been so serious at the beginning of the trip. "Want to play?" he asked Clara after Hadley had beaten him again.

"But you always win, Papa."

"Not always. But I try."

"Then I want to play the Wonder Woman machine." Her eyes squeezed shut with excitement.

"You could beat me at that one."

"I think she's counting on that, Jurgen." Hadley drew closer to watch.

Chapter 24

Getting ready for New Year's Eve, Hadley was a mess. Her makeup had taken half an hour. She didn't want to get any on her dress, so she was being very careful. This would be her final night on the ship. They'd spent the day on the top deck playing games, sipping hot chocolate and eating potato pancakes and schnitzel. What could be better?

But she knew she would feel very sad when it came time to leave tomorrow. That sadness came over her in unexpected waves. Watching Clara play darts, with Jurgen helping her aim. Seeing Emerson and Aunt Ethel teasing each other about which waffles were better…American or Belgian. And then looking up to find Jurgen's dark eyes on her. She would take home wonderful memories. But would that be enough?

"Knock, knock," her aunt sang out.

Hadley opened the door. "Come on in. I need help zipping up the back. Oh, my gosh. Look at you."

Her aunt swept inside looking beautiful in a shimmering black gown with the emerald necklace. "You look fabulous. But I feel terrible that you can't wear the earrings to go with that necklace."

When her aunt lifted her hair back from her ears, Hadley

screamed. "You are kidding me! They found it?"

"Oh yes," her aunt said, turning her head in Hadley's mirror so she could better appreciate the earrings. "Fritz knows the chief of security at the opera house."

"Wait a minute. Who's Fritz?" Sometimes it was hard to follow her aunt.

"Emerson!" Her aunt continued to fuss with her hair. "His name is Fritz Emerson."

"Oh, right." So it was that serious between them.

"Anyway," her aunt continued. "They turned the opera house upside down. The earring was found in the carpet near the third-floor restroom. Isn't that amazing?" Her aunt laughed but for Hadley this wasn't funny.

"Thank goodness. I can hardly believe it." She was so relieved that the precious earring hadn't been vacuumed up. From now on, she was wearing pierced earrings only.

Her aunt made a circular motion with one hand. "Now turn around so I can see how this looks."

After Aunt Ethel had zipped up the back of the dress, she also fastened the tiny covered buttons along the spine. "You can always tell the quality of a gown by the little things. I look for covered buttons. These are done beautifully. That Elka, she is something else. There, now. Look at yourself."

"Oh, wow." Hadley turned in front of the mirror, loving the way the fabric rustled against her legs. The bodice fit perfectly. She held out her arms so Aunt Ethel could fasten the buttons at the wrist of both sleeves.

"Lovely. In every way, my dear. Should I help you with the necklace?"

"Yes, please." The case was set out on the dressing table. It didn't take two seconds for Aunt Ethel to fasten the beautifully designed piece around her neck while Hadley attached the earrings. The blue stones glistened against the luminous fabric that looked like moonlight. She could hardly speak.

Was this really her standing there in the mirror, her dark eyes sparkling? The front of her hair was swept up, with long curls left in the back. Perfect for showcasing the earrings. "Have I used too much of that smoky shadow on my eyes?"

"Not at all." Aunt Ethel leaned closer to Hadley's mirror. "Maybe I should put on more eyeshadow myself."

"I think you look fine. But do whatever you're comfortable with."

But her aunt had gone back to fluffing her hair. She couldn't remember when Aunt Ethel had taken this much time with herself. "I'm just thankful that you're in a better place now. Brock didn't deserve you. Not after what you told me last night about your assistant."

"That's a real disappointment. But I should've been paying more attention. While I was busy closing deals and looking for the next prospect, Miranda was stealing my fiancé."

"I'm sure you won't make that mistake again."

Hadley slipped into her heels. "Again? I don't think there'll be an 'again.' Not anytime soon anyway."

"Well, we'll just see about that, won't we? I want to see the look on Jurgen's face when he sees you."

"The Crown Prince. This is beginning to feel like a fairytale."

"Oh, I hope so."

"Do you think Emerson could snap a few photos?"

"Fritz? Absolutely. Speaking of photos, who do you think took that shot of the two of you at the opera house? That was quite a little story. And they had some details about you too. 'Chicago Mover and Shaker.' Made me proud."

Turning, Hadley snatched up her little clutch. "I've been wondering that myself. Do you think it was one of the security guards?"

"Could be. They may have felt that they were on their way out. And that picture probably brought whoever sold it to the media a pretty penny."

"I'd like to get a copy of it, if I just knew who to ask."

"I'll ask Fritz," her aunt said as she walked out into the salon. For a second, they both stood there, taking in their beautiful Christmas tree. "I hate to turn off the tree lights. This has been such a wonderful holiday. I don't want to see it end."

"Me too." Going to the window, Hadley stared out at the river. The huge Parliament Building was alight, setting the dark river on fire with its gold and orange reflection. "This is so beautiful. I'd like to come back someday."

"I'm sure you will," her aunt said with quiet assurance. "As for myself, I don't know when I've had a more entertaining time."

"Well, besides…" Hadley was sure this didn't compare to the trips with her uncle.

"No, I mean ever. Why, with everything that was going on with Jurgen and Clara, there was never a boring moment. And it isn't over."

And with that, they turned out the lights and left the room.

***

"Dinner was so good. I feel like I might burst," she told Jurgen as he took her in his arms for the first waltz. "I haven't eaten roast pork in a long time."

"It's supposed to be a lucky meal." He smiled down on her. "The pork fat symbolizes wealth."

"What about the lentil soup?" The choice of soup had surprised her.

"Same thing. The more lentils you eat, the richer you will be in the coming year.'

"Maybe I should have eaten more."

"I'd say you did all right with the *Tim Tam Pavlova* and the *Buche de Noel*."

"I couldn't choose." She groaned. "The stacked meringues and the cake roll both looked so good."

"And you shouldn't have to. Not on New Year's Eve." Jurgen had been so serious tonight. She didn't know what to think. But he sure looked handsome in that tuxedo. "Are you ready to dance?"

The area used for karaoke had been cleared and set up as a ballroom for tonight. Small candles glowed on the tables. Balloons bobbled against the ceiling and the entire room was decorated in blue and silver. The orchestra began the waltz.

Putting her left hand on Jurgen's shoulder, Hadley hoped those

YouTube videos came to her aid now. Over the past two days, she'd been practicing waltzing by viewing videos at any opportunity.

"You're quite stunning tonight," Jurgen told her as they circled the dance floor.

"So are you." She tried to keep count of their steps in her head.

"I'm stunning?" He grinned. "I'm more stunned… by you."

"Maybe. Please don't confuse me. I'm counting."

"Let me lead. No need to count." He was a very good dancer.

"Let you lead?" she teased. "Are you kidding? You don't know me very well."

"I'm hoping you give me the chance to know you better," he whispered against her forehead.

These vague comments he'd been making all evening left her feeling nervous. For Hadley, it was easier to end things and walk away. But where had that gotten her in the past?

"Now, don't get all serious." Jurgen tightened his hold on her waist. "Smile when we pass Clara. I gave her my phone to take pictures."

"Is she good at that?" All kinds of questions popped up in her head.

"You know how precocious she is."

"But you don't think…"

He seemed to miss a beat for a second. "That never occurred to me. But perhaps I should check my phone." They picked up their rhythm. The waltz felt so freeing with its sweeping steps. But she wished she hadn't worn these high heels.

"I think I should have worn a lower heel. Maybe two inches or so."

"Your heels are perfect. And I'd like to see more of them." Then he flushed. "By that I mean a shorter skirt."

"Uh huh. Just remember, Clara is watching."

"I know." And he sighed as she laughed.

The number ended and Jurgen executed a polite little bow. Then he led her to the table where Ethel sat, along with Emerson, Miss Schmidt and Clara. The orchestra was beginning another waltz and Jurgen turned to his daughter. "And now if I could have the honor."

"Oh yes, Papa!" She was on her feet in a moment, and the two of them danced off. Thank goodness she was wearing the red and green taffeta dress. The jingle bells under her red dress would have given the orchestra some competition. Clara was quite a bit shorter than Jurgen but somehow they managed.

"Such a beautiful pair," Aunt Ethel said as Jurgen and Clara circled the floor.

"Yes, Clara dances quite well. I wonder if she took lessons."

"Hadley, I'm talking about you and Jurgen."

"Oh. Us." She didn't know what to say. Since they lived in different countries, anything beyond these two weeks would be very complicated. Jurgen probably realized that. So instead, she thought ahead to her return to Chicago. Picking up her career while she looked for another assistant wouldn't be easy. But she wouldn't worry about that now.

***

Midnight was approaching. Most of the guests were gathered on the top deck, waiting for the fireworks to be set off over the Danube. Waiters circulated with trays of champagne. Thank goodness it wasn't windy tonight. The air was cold and still and Hadley was bundled in one of the warm blankets.

Clara had fallen asleep in the seating area and Jurgen had left her cuddled next to Emerson and Aunt Ethel. "If I take her down to our suite, she'll be mad that she missed the fireworks."

"It feels good to be off my feet," Aunt Ethel said. Emerson had his arm around her.

Other guests stood or were seated in clusters, some sipping warm wine or cider instead of the champagne. On the screen the staff had projected New Year's Eve as it happened around the globe, by time zone. "Almost our turn," Hadley said watching the hand move.

Coming up behind her, Jurgen wrapped his arms tight around her. Even though she was leaving, this felt so good. Countdown numbers flashed on the screen, with the crowd joining in.

Then sirens wailed and fireworks crackled across the dark sky. When she turned, Jurgen tilted her head back. "Happy New Year, my love." And he kissed her. She became lost in that kiss. When Brock had used "my love" with her in an email, it had felt phony. But not with Jurgen. He meant it. And she felt those words in her heart.

"Don't leave," he whispered. "Come home with me. See my country. See the real me."

Shocking as it was, the idea appealed to her. "But I should get back to work."

He sighed with such disappointment. She saw it in his eyes. Felt it under her palms, resting on his chest. "To your old life?"

"Yes." No, she didn't want that.

"Just think about it," he said, kissing her forehead. "You don't have to leave tomorrow. This ship has a week in Budapest before leaving. Stay and we can talk about our next steps. Please, Hadley. I love you so and you know Clara does too."

"Happy New Year!" Then Aunt Ethel was at her elbow. Everyone was hugging and celebrating, while overhead, the sky exploded in every color imaginable. Clara woke up and her father scooped her up into his arms. Together they watched the sky and Hadley knew she would never have another night like this. Knew that for her, there would never be another man like Jurgen Lundborg…or whatever his name really was.

Her answer had to be yes. There was no other way.

Epilogue

One Year Later

Never did Hadley ever think she would be married on New Year's Day, and yet it felt right. Jurgen had suggested this date months ago. For them, the Christmas market cruise and the ship would always be their special place and time of year. By noon, all the passengers had left. Her family was up on the top deck, playing cornhole with the kids. Well, the dads were. Most of the women were probably getting ready for the wedding.

They would be married at eight o'clock, followed by a sit-down dinner that ended in dancing. Ballroom dancing. Leanne and Mindy were so excited about that and Clara was too, of course. Amber had taken Clara under her wing the moment the family arrived. And Clara delighted in showing her the ship. By that time they were old friends, since Jurgen had brought Clara to Chicago to visit.

Last September her mother had come to Prague with Aunt Ethel to help Hadley find a wedding dress at Elka's shop. He mother was almost beside herself when Daddy told her that of course she should go when the topic was broached.

Since last Christmas, Hadley had come for extended vacations in Starengard. But every time she left, it became more and more difficult to leave Jurgen and Clara. Oh, sure, there had been other meetings, like the week in Paris and one in London. Aunt Ethel had provided Hadley with information on where to go and what to see. Hadley wanted Clara to enjoy the arts in the great cites as much as she did. Jurgen watched them with affection as they were ushered around by security.

Meeting Jurgen's mother had been by far the most nerve-wracking trip to Starengard. And yet, Hadley could see that the Queen wanted only the best for her son and granddaughter. She was grateful when Queen Elise asked if Hadley would like her to arrange some lessons in royal protocols. The Queen intended to step down within the next five years.

Hadley had wound down her business in Chicago and sold her condo. For the past three months, she'd lived here, more certain than ever that, as unlikely as it might be, this was the only place for her now. This was the man she wanted at her side for the rest of her life.

When a knock came at the door, it was Aunt Ethel. They'd agreed that she would stay in the Royal Suite with Hadley just as she had one year ago. In a move to accommodate the market, Jurgen had made Executive Suites out of half the rooms on the second floor. The new suites turned out to be the first to be reserved as soon as they went live online. Hadley had helped with the planning and the decorating. And for this past week, her family had been occupying some of the suites, enjoying the Christmas market cruise.

"Your mother will be here in a moment," Aunt Ethel said, swirling into the room in a lavender dress she'd ordered from Elka.

"My dress is over on the mannequin." And Hadley led Aunt Ethel back into her bedroom.

"You will be a beautiful bride." Aunt Ethel stood back as if to take in the sight. "Oh my dear, I can hardly believe this but it seems so right"

Hadley nodded. "I know. When I said yes to you a year ago, I didn't know what I was saying yes to."

"Sometimes a yes is waiting for us," Aunt Ethel whispered. "Just waiting until we know it is right." Her blissful expression made Hadley wonder if Aunt Ethel had any wedding plans with Emerson, who was such a wonderful man.

Another knock came at the door and Hadley rushed to let her mother in.

***

The orchestra began to play Pachelbel's Canon. Everyone had been seated in the ballroom filled with the white calla lilies and freesia Hadley had wanted for this day.

Mindy began her walk, followed by Leanne. Mindy's boys actually were quiet, maybe stunned to see their mom in her long lavender gown. Leanne looked so relaxed. After leaving their toddler with a sitter, Steve and Leanne were enjoying a bit of a holiday.

Lastly came Clara, wearing a dress similar to Hadley's. The same lace, the same sleeves, but a smaller, more delicate bouquet. Her beautiful hair was caught back in curls as she tossed white rose petals. Snapping at the petals, Shatzi caused a bit of a stir, straining at the leash Emerson held as they walked up the aisle. The lace-edged cushion on Shatzi's back marked her as the ring bearer. Fritz Emerson—Hadley still had trouble with that name—served as Jurgen's best man.

As Hadley stood waiting on her father's arm, Jurgen looked past the approaching wedding party. Dressed in his military whites, he looked more handsome than the prince in any fairytale. She'd have to ask him later to explain the many medals that decorated his chest, as well as the sash.

Breathless. This man left her breathless. His truth, his goodness and his love had been shown to her in so many ways over the past year. She smiled at him standing there, waiting patiently. Clara had to go over to whisper something to him before taking her place with Mindy and Leanne.

The walk wasn't long. Just a few notes. A few steps. When she reached Jurgen, Daddy lifted Hadley's veil and kissed her cheek. Oh, it hadn't been easy to convince her father. He hadn't wanted her to leave home until he saw her with Jurgen and Clara. "They need you," Daddy had told her. "And I think you need them too, sweetheart. Does the palace have a carving set?"

Jurgen had laughed at that. They hadn't opened all the wedding gifts yet, but she was pretty sure she knew what was in one of those boxes. Turning, she spotted Aunt Ethel in the front row with

Mom. Of course they both were crying,

"My darling Princess Hadley of Starengard," Jurgen whispered. She smiled up into her future. Just a few kisses into forever. And she could hardly wait for their new journey to begin.

THE END

Be sure to sign up for Barbara's newsletter for an alert about other books in the *Romancing the Royals* series. Go to:

www.BarbaraLohrAuthor.com
www.facebook.com/barbaralohrauthor

Other Books by Barbara Lohr

Romancing the Royals

The Royal Governess
Heiress In Training
The Christmas Cruise

Best Friends to Forever

Marry Me, Jackson
Steal My Heart, Trevor
Christmas with Dr. Darling

Man from Yesterday series

Coming Home to You
Always on His Mind
In His Eyes
Late Bloomer
Still Not Over You
Every Breath You Take
Christmas Dreams and Santa Schemes

Windy City Romance series

Finding Southern Comfort
Her Favorite Mistake
Her Favorite Honeymoon
Her Favorite Hot Doc
The Christmas Baby Bundle
Rescuing the Reluctant Groom
The Southern Comfort Christmas

About the Author

Barbara Lohr writes sweet contemporary romance. She lives in the South of the United States with her husband and a cat that insists he was Heathcliff in another life. Visit her Facebook page and be sure to sign up for her newsletter for new releases, great giveaways and a fun group of readers who enjoy Barbara's work.

www.BarbaraLohrAuthor.com
www.facebook.com/Barbaralohrauthor
www.twitter.com/BarbaraJLohr

Made in the USA
Coppell, TX
22 September 2023